Mermaid's Key

Amanda Mahan

Black Rose Writing | Texas

ISBN: 978-1-68433-389-9
PUBLISHED BY BLACK ROSE WRITING
www.blackrosewriting.com

Printed in the United States of America
Suggested Retail Price (SRP) $16.95

Mermaid's Key is printed in Chaparral Pro
Author photo courtesy of Deo Greene

*The final word count for this book may not match your standard expectation versus
the final page count. In an effort to reduce paper usage and energy costs, Black Rose
Writing, as a planet-friendly publisher, does its best to eliminate unnecessary waste
without lessening your reading experience.

Acknowledgements

I extend my deepest thanks to my dear friends and family who have given me great support, confidence, cheering, and love over the many years needed to complete this project. To my first readers - my sister Anna and my dad Gary, thank you slogging through a rough idea and still believing in me enough to encourage me to continue. To both my parents, thank you for everything, including your unconditional love and dedication. To Michael, your words of encouragement have always been delivered at just the right moments. It's because of Susan that I wrote this book to the end and then kept on pushing to publication - you never let me quit. Thanks to Haidyn and Mika for being my first young adult readers and giving it a thumbs up. Al, thanks for telling me early on that my story was worth writing. Thanks Fletcher, for showing me it can be done and spurring me to do so. Ms. Cosby, thank you for teaching me to love books in 11th grade. Sarah, thank you for loving with the biggest heart and setting the highest bar for mothering, goodness, and friendship - I based the mom on you. Rebeccah, thanks for dreaming far and wide with me all the time. Nancy, you pushed me to manifest this book into being - thank you. Laura, thanks for always listening and holding me up with your wise insights. Leah, thanks for making me want to read because you always were and for being my lifelong friend. Stacy, I'm so thankful for your faithful friendship and support. To Holland, I love that you write mermaid stories too and can't wait to explore the worlds you create. Marla, thanks for placing every comma and moving every adverb, in the briefest of time, during the busiest of days - you make me look good. James, you gave me the story, the space to write, and the support to keep trying - thank you, thank you, thank you. Eli and Deo, thanks for making me a mom, teaching me the most profound understanding of love, and telling me again and again that I'm good - I wrote this book for you. I hope you both travel the world and beyond like Evan and Ross.

Mermaid's Key

Prologue

The thick, hot air pressed in against her, making it hard to breathe. She took short, sharp breaths, but the weight of the air made it feel as though she was drowning on dry land. Her skin crisped in the oven around her. She felt as if she might ignite if it weren't for the heavy humidity squeezing upon her and the sweat seeping from every pore. She was blinded not from total darkness, but from complete brightness instead. Turning her face away from the flaming sun towards the dry, hot sand at her feet, she squinted, rapidly blinking away tears. Streams streaked down her cheeks. The warm liquid felt cool in comparison to the burn blistering underneath. She closed her eyes and held them tightly sealed. The fluorescent orange light seared through her lids, the hot light still blinding. Opening her eyes into slight slits, she struggled to look around. All she could make out were dark shapes sharply contrasted with the flooding light. She held her hand to her hairline trying to shield, but it was no use. The bright white light still blazed her eyes and scorched her pale face. She attempted to take a long calming breath, but the air felt too hot as it filled her lungs, boiling her from within.

So this was the surface. She was wrong to have come.

Chapter 1

The crumbs of dead coral coarsely ground into a fine gravel crunched and shifted under Evan's feet. "Some beach," he scoffed, insulted by the lack of sand. He had anticipated the smooth white beaches pictured in magazines, but instead, he was presented with a beach littered with rotting seaweed the color of mustard and smelling much worse. The sand was rough and uneven, the hue of dead skin, and that's practically what he was walking on now - the crushed skeletons of former sea life, once colorfully swaying below the surface. The thought caused a wave of chill to wash over him despite the intense heat of the afternoon sun. The oppressive humidity dampened every inch of his clothing. The water had not even provided relief from the heat since it was as hot as a bath. He hated it here.

As he stomped down the beach, a sharp edge unexpectedly jabbed his sole, which only inflamed him more. Evan kicked at the shoreline, wishing he could inflict pain or damage that would compare to the volume of frustration he felt. Here he was again, alone in some corner of the world, wanting someone, anyone, to be his friend.

"Come on Evan, this is paradise," his mom tried to convince him. "Other kids would kill to spend their afternoon on the beach instead of in school." She would say the same about a mountain peak or canyon or tropical rainforest or desert valley or wherever his parents' latest assignment had taken them. He was expected to be happy about his freedom to explore and his privilege of exposure. "What kid wouldn't want to travel the world rather than live in some boring town and attend some normal school?" his parents would ask. However, he resented his parents' work and came to dread the constant travel. He didn't want to visit another quaint foreign village, hike another exotic jungle trail or spend hours in museums viewing masterpieces. No one had asked him if this was the life he wanted. The way he saw it, he was far from Shangri-la. He often thought of sitting at a classroom desk in some suburban public high school, listening to a mediocre teacher lecture on a topic he had studied several years earlier. That might be his utopia instead. At least then, he might be able to pass a note, send a text, or meet friends at the park for a game of pickup basketball. Maybe he could make plans for later in the afternoon to ride bikes down some street lined with cookie-cutter houses or hang out at some stale mall. He would choose that over this "paradise" any day.

In that ordinary teenage world, Evan might have a friend. The closest thing to a friend he had now was Ross. On paper, he was the perfect brother. He wasn't the usual pesky kid inserting himself where he didn't belong; instead, he always respected Evan's space. Ross was understanding and continually calm, even when Evan would lose his temper and lash out at him. He had everything that Evan wished he had more of - patience, thoughtfulness and an undampened sense of humor. Ross was adventurous and up for anything, always seeking out new experiences for them to share. He was even a challenging classmate, pushing Evan to question a little deeper rather than accepting the easiest explanation. He was also close enough in age to be placed in the friend category - just 11 months younger. However, Ross was not what Evan needed in a friend. It was pretty hard to be friends with someone who refused to talk.

While their parents were on a recent assignment photographing the cliffs at Halong Bay in the South China Sea off the coast of Vietnam, Evan and Ross were studying Buddhist monks as part of their independent coursework. After visiting a temple where a group of monks had not spoken for 20 years, Ross had become so enthralled by the practice of silence that he too decided to make his own vow and give up speaking. Evan thought that after a few days, at most a month, his brother wouldn't be able to stand it any longer and would speak again, but it had been four and half months, 139 days to be exact, and Ross still hadn't said a word, not even when provoked. Evan had tried everything from bad jokes, taunts, threats, bribes, even jabs, and a few shoves, but Ross still wouldn't speak. Not a peep. His discipline was resolute. Evan felt alone, without anyone to talk to, except to their exhausted parents over dinners late at night. It was not really what he was looking for in the way of friendship.

Ross had always been that way. Even as a young boy, when he put his mind to something, he would not relinquish his commitment until he reached his goal. He was the most determined person Evan knew, never losing focus. At ten years old, Ross decided that he would eat raw food exclusively for a full year. Their parents had been working a story on the seals in the San Francisco Bay and as usual, Evan and Ross were left alone for the day to explore. The brothers wandered the city, having breakfast of sourdough bread and chocolates at the wharf, followed by a walk up the hills to some of the trendier neighborhoods. After several hours of aimless hiking up and down the undulating sidewalks, Ross chose a small outdoor café in the shadow of Coit Tower, with a view of Alcatraz, to have their lunch. Evan had selected their breakfast location, so he didn't get to object to Ross' obscure choice now, even though it didn't appeal to him at all. It was an all-raw restaurant serving up fermented salads and unbaked "muffins." After reading on the menu that cooking food reduced the vitamin content, that was enough to convince Ross. He didn't eat anything cooked for the rest of the year. He read countless books and articles, espousing the virtues of a raw diet. He sprouted seeds and beans and dehydrated pureed vegetables and fruits to make what the recipe books claimed to be alternatives to crackers. While Evan tried to taunt him by waving a crisp, warm fry in front of his brother's face and taking a huge bite out of a juicy cheeseburger, dripping with savory cooked goodness, Ross would resolutely and contentedly sip on his own tepid soup, which Evan had rudely called baby food. But nothing phased Ross. At ten, he had as much self-restraint and willpower as an athlete preparing for the Olympics. He was focused on his goal and never cheated once.

Because of this, Evan now had little hope of his brother returning to the land of the speaking any time soon. Ross had committed himself to silence, and no one was sure how long it might last. He had not mouthed a single word to Evan, to their parents, to anyone, and Evan missed their brotherly banter that they would volley while walking or riding bikes. He longed for one of Ross' quick-witted comments about a stranger passing by as they sat on the curb of a busy street. At this point, he would even settle for a conversation about their schoolwork - anything that would get his brother talking again. At night, in the dark quiet just before sleep, he wished he and his brother would still make plans for the following day in a hushed whisper or recount silly lines from their favorite movies. Some days the silence would drive Evan mad, and he would carry on a conversation for Ross. He would ask his brother a question and then respond in a mocking voice meant to imitate Ross, often carrying on in this manner for several minutes. Ross would only silently roll his eyes at Evan's absurdity.

Alone without even his brother for a friend, in this so-called paradise, this poor excuse for a beach half-way down the chain of islands that comprised the

Florida Keys, Evan half-stomped, half-stumbled along the shoreline, cursing his current situation. He wished he had grabbed his flip-flops before storming out from their hotel room. When he had asked Ross if he wanted to take out one of the kayaks at the hotel to explore the cove, Ross had only shrugged in the negative and went back to reading. Evan had pleaded, "Come on man, just for an hour. I'm sick of working on this unit. Let's go see what's around the other side of the island." But again, Ross merely shook his head and gave Evan a blank-looking face in response. He could understand that Ross wasn't speaking, but he couldn't stand what seemed to be a complete emotional void in his brother. As Evan's furry boiled hotter, Ross seemed to turn his emotions even cooler.

"God, you act like a lifeless robot!" Evan had screamed on the way out the door. He had stomped off, without grabbing shoes and headed down the breezeway lined with hotel doors and humming air conditioning units. He had cursed under his breath when he passed the colorful kayaks lined up on the shore. The reds, blues and greens of the faded plastic hulls looked like a postcard he had seen in the spinning rack at the tacky hotel tourist giftshop. He picked up a chunk of gravel from the hotel parking lot and threw it at the offending red hull but missed. His anger flamed like wildfire and was matched by the searing temperature of the tarmac that charred his feet while crossing US Highway 1. His soles felt tender and raw now as they rubbed against the grainy sand of the beach.

The blue-green water of the Atlantic Ocean gently lapped along the shore where the large clumps of rotting seaweed, baked in the sun. As Evan trudged across the damp, spongy clutter that littered the coarse, gravelly sand, its sour smell was released like a scratch-and-sniff sticker. "This beach sucks," he mumbled. At that moment, something more jagged than sand stabbed the arch of his foot, causing him to stumble to the ground. He cursed again before checking to see that his foot wasn't bleeding. He then looked behind him to find what had made him fall.

Two dark teeth protruded from the light sand. On his hands and knees, he brushed the sand and seaweed away from the object, revealing an ancient key. It looked like something from a mythical shipwreck. Measuring almost the full length of his hand, the key felt heavy for its size. The metal was old but free from rust, corrosion or barnacles. It obviously had not been lying on the bottom of the ocean for centuries. Instead, it was like this key had been kept in a glass case inside a museum. It was polished and shining. The shaft end was simple with two thick tines, like those on an old skeleton key. Evan was unsure of the metal and marveled at how brightly it shined. Could it be solid gold, he wondered? The bow end was ornately decorated, studded with glowing, opalescent pearls and thin wisps of looping metal. It vaguely reminded Evan of Celtic knots, but its motif was certainly distinct from that. He couldn't place its design in the timeline of art history, unsure of how old it could be. It was unlike anything he had ever seen. Captivated by its beauty, he stroked the cool metal and stared at the treasure in his hand, imagining what door this key might unlock.

Chapter 2

At dinner that night, Evan mindlessly stirred his ketchup with a fry, lost in thought. Picturing a large wooden treasure chest with an ornate lock that his newly discovered key might fit, he imagined his hand trembling as it held the heavy key ready to insert it. As he turned the shaft, the key easily rotated in the slot. The curved lid moaned as he lifted it, releasing the musty smell of clay and rotting earth, revealing the glimmering contents from within.

"Earth to Evan. Come in Evan. Over," his dad teased. "What are you thinking about, buddy?" he asked, looking at him from across the table. Evan gazed down at his ketchup-covered fry and shook his head, blinking back to the present.

"Oh, nothing, Dad."

"Come on, Evan. You were a hundred miles away. It had to have been something good." His dad stretched his arms behind his head and arched his back over the top edge of his chair, releasing a loud pop from his chest, followed by a relieved sigh. "I've been working all day. Your mom had me crawling at the oddest angles to get the most perfect shot for her piece." He winked lovingly at his wife sitting next to him and squeezed her knee under the table as she rolled her eyes in mocking exaggeration. Looking back to Evan, he continued, "I'm beat and could use a good story. Plus, this guy isn't going to crack," his dad said as he winked and gestured with his thumb towards Ross, who gave a half-smile in response. "Tell us what has you floating away, lost so deeply in thought."

Evan felt possessive, wanting his discovery to be his own. He knew that if he showed the key to his parents, they would instantly want to take it to some professor-friend at some museum or university so that it could be analyzed and archived. "This is an important find, Evan," his mom would say as she peered over the edge of her reading glasses. "It needs to be studied. Documented." His dad, of course, would first want to photograph it before sending it off and his mom might pitch it as a story for the magazine, but the key surely wouldn't be left to him to keep.

Evan selfishly wanted more time with it. He enjoyed the mystery surrounding it and liked imagining what it may unlock. Since stumbling upon it, the weight of the key in his hand had lightened his mood. He had spent the afternoon, walking around the island, rubbing his fingers over the elegant curves and looped metal, stroking the silky cool pearls. He imagined the key fitting into all manner of locks - a pirate's treasure, a captain's ship door, the hope chest of a princess or a secret chamber in an abbey on a remote island. But all of these possibilities seemed absurd and trivial for a key of its kind. There was something about this key that was magical, otherworldly even, convincing him its potential was far greater than any of those more mundane purposes. He felt compelled to know what secrets it held. In the short time, he had it, the key had possessed him, held some power over him, and he felt protective of it. This was his treasure, and he didn't want it to be sent off for analysis and documentation, at least not yet.

Also, he was still mad at his taciturn brother, and the last thing he wanted was to share this adventure with him. He refused to let Ross sit silently by while he confided this with him. If Ross were talking, Evan knew that his brother would conjure the most elaborate scenarios about what this key was and where it might be from. Ross would describe in richly glowing detail the size of a massive door in which this key might fit and craft an entire civilization around it. Ross would recount the legend of the man who might have forged the key hundreds of years before, the secret society that had been sworn to protect it and the contents it kept securely locked. In the next breath, he would tell a tale of a beautiful maiden locked high in a tower while a knight combed the countryside, searching for this lost key which would set her free. Ross was a master of constructing stories, and that was what Evan had missed most during this season of silence. Evan was darn sure he wasn't going to allow Ross the satisfaction of creating a grand saga surrounding his key, and keep it silently to himself.

Everyone at the table was staring at him, waiting for him to say something. Evan lacked his brother's quick-witted ability to create entertaining stories, so he was unable to concoct an alternate account about how he had spent his day. Additionally, he was without Ross' self-control, so he couldn't restrain himself. He was just too excited about his discovery to remain silent. Like with all of his emotions, it bubbled up and overcame him. He blurted out impulsively, "I found a key on the beach today."

"What do you mean, a key? Like a boat key or something?" his dad asked in a puzzled tone.

Immediately cursing his impetuous confession, he reluctantly pulled his prize from his pocket and extended his hand across the table. The large pearls on the gilded end of the key seemed to glow in the soft light of the restaurant. Upon looking at it again and validated by the gaze of others, Evan realized it really was an impressive object that seemed to exude some mythical quality. Seeing it in contrast against the red and white checkered pattern of the plastic coated tablecloth, it looked as though it was from another world, or at least from another time.

"Oh my," his mother said, drawing in her breath. "It's exquisite. Where did you find it? On the beach? Just out there? Really?" his mother rattled on as she reached her fingers to lightly trace the length of the key. Evan could see the power of the key luring her to it, laying its claim upon her as it had him. "May I hold it?" she asked in a hushed tone, as one might ask to hold a newborn.

"Yeah, I guess you can," Evan said bitterly, granting her permission to examine the key more closely. He reluctantly pushed it closer towards his mom as he felt himself deflate. He knew it, he should have never brought it out. "I just found it out on the beach this afternoon. I actually stepped on it and fell when it poked me in the foot."

Delicately holding the key in both hands, his mom lifted it to eye level to examine it more closely. "We should let Steve Winston have a look at this and see if he's seen anything like it before," she said as she slightly tilted her head towards his father, indicating that he should contact his old college friend. Just like Evan had predicted. He rolled his eyes and exhaled loudly. Unfazed by Evan's irritation, she rotated the artifact in her hands, studying the looped metal as if she were trying to decipher an ancient text. She brought it to her mouth and to Evan's shock, gently bit one the pearls between her front teeth. "It's perfect. These pearls are real and flawless... so big. I've never seen anything like it. Really, Evan, we need to have this analyzed by an expert, and Steve's the right guy for the job. He's an archeologist whose work focuses on oceanic artifacts. Plus, he's close by, just up the road in Miami. We could swing by his office before we fly out in two days." Evan rolled his eyes again. His mom was already making plans to have his discovery studied at some university lab. Evan snatched the key back.

"Come on Mom. I found it, and I'm keeping it." Evan embarrassed himself by how loudly he had yelled at her in the restaurant, which caused people at nearby tables to look their way. He glanced around apologetically at the other diners, who politely returned their attention to their meals. All except one. Evan shifted in his chair, turning his back slightly to the table just beside them to block the view of the old man who sat next to them. The man had been staring at them the entire evening, not only just after his recent outburst. Evan had noticed him when he walked into the restaurant shortly after they had been seated because his appearance seemed so cliché. He was dressed like a salty sea-dog captain character from an old television show. He even had a navy cap, torn striped shirt, and burly white beard, plus a pipe dangling from his mouth. He had been seated at the table beside theirs. To see him sitting alone in a seafood restaurant with fishing nets, ship's wheels and old barometers decorating the walls, it was as if he was part of the kitsch ornamentation too. However, the guy was starting to creep Evan out. The man made no attempt to hide the fact that he had been watching them since he had taken his seat at the table beside them. Evan had wondered what this guy's deal was early on but had shrugged off his feeling that this guy had followed them into the restaurant. Yet, since Evan had revealed his treasure to his family, the old man hadn't removed his gaze from the key. The intensity of his stare had caught the attention of Ross as well, who positioned his body to block the man's view and protect his family's discussion.

"Evan, simmer down. Please don't speak to me that way." His mother's reprimand was gentle as always, causing Evan to feel shame at his outburst. "And besides, you know that ownership isn't merely based on a finders keepers system," his mom added. His parents had always spoken to Ross and Evan in a calm, tempered way. It was kind and loving, but also was one of the things that drove Evan mad about them and made him feel even more different from them, alienated by his unbridled emotions. They never seemed angry or ruffled. When Evan had broken a window with a baseball, his dad hadn't shouted but instead coolly said, "Man, what a bummer. Evan, what are your plans for fixing this?" When Evan pushed his brother out of frustration during one of their many childhood squabbles, his mom would say, "No thank you. We treat everyone with respect and control only our own bodies." They never yelled, and it made Evan feel crazy. He was the only one in the family who seemed to have a temper, and that only fueled his rage further.

Yet, here it was again. The same speech about collecting. While other kids were allowed to pick flowers during a hike in the woods, gather rocks from a creek bed or collect seashells, Evan and Ross had been taught that the only thing they could take were photographs. Since his parents prided themselves on being conservators of the natural world, they were strict in their principles of being guardians rather than collectors or exploiters, as they often dismissively described others in their field. His mom was a writer, and his dad a photographer. They had met 20 years before while on assignment for National Geographic. During the years since, while traversing the planet for their work, the boys were never allowed to keep souvenirs. Naturally, this didn't seem to bother Ross, as it seemed nothing did. However, Evan was often left disappointed and even heart-broken by the policy.

He remembered being seven and having to leave behind a small salamander he had found in a mountain stream. He had played with the little creature the entire day, building a protected habitat for him, stockpiling bugs and crayfish for him to eat. He had held the little fellow, stroking his smooth, cool skin, becoming attached, falling deeper and deeper into his emotions for his new "friend." Meanwhile, Ross had collected and categorized rocks found in the same stream, laying them along its bank by the classifications he had just learned - sedimentary, igneous and metamorphic. After his parents had gotten the story and the accompanying photographs and it was time to leave, Evan was crushed that he couldn't take the salamander with him. "But I promise I'll take good care of him, Mom," he had pleaded.

She only responded calmly, "Oh, no sweetheart, he belongs here with his family."

While tears streamed down Evan's cheeks, Ross simply turned and walked away from his precisely stacked piles of rocks without even thinking about slipping his favorite into his pocket. Every time Evan saw a salamander in a stream, zoo, or pet shop since he would have to turn away and fight back a wave that would rise from the well deep within.

He also recalled the beautiful crystal he had found in a cavern in Mexico. He was eleven, and his family planned a day excursion after his parents wrapped up another assignment. They arranged for a guide to take them into a cavern known for its remarkable crystal formations. Evan had ventured off alone down a short corridor while the rest of his family sat for a short water break. It was like the glowing shaft had been left for him to find, lying directly before him on the path. He had rushed back with his treasure, so excited to show his discovery to his mom, "Look at this! Can you believe it? It's the length of my hand and as big around as my wrist! It looks like chiseled ice!" His mother had kneeled beside him and placed her hand gently on his shoulder as they examined the crystal. They marveled at how the light refracted when they held it to their headlamps. They giggled at the upturned world they saw when they looked through it. "Can I keep it Mom, please?" Evan had begged.

His mother shook her head and lightly rubbed his back, as she said, "No, honey. This crystal is of this world and is meant to stay here. Just think of the next person who will have the joy of discovering this like we did."

Evan had wanted to throw the crystal to the ground, shattering it, so no one else could see it's beauty, but before he could, his mother had scooped it from his hands and replaced it exactly where he had found it. "It's not yours to take, my dear."

Nothing ever was, and now his mom was saying that to him again. "Evan, just because you found the key, it doesn't make it yours," she said before taking another bite of her salad.

"But, Mom..." Evan started. He knew there wasn't anything he could say to convince her that he should keep the key. He should have kept his mouth shut like his brother. He glared at Ross, feeling like he was somehow silently complicit in ruining his treasure as well, but Ross only softened his expression towards Evan, clearly communicating that he empathized with his brother's loss. Evan huffed out a hot breath and looked down at his now empty hands. He should have kept the key his secret.

"Evan, your mom is right. We really need to let someone study this remarkable find," his dad added as he reached to take the key from his wife's hand. His dad also marveled at the object's beauty as he stroked the length of the smooth metal and fingered the uniquely cut tines. "I wonder what type of metal it's made from and how old it could possibly be? It seems ancient." He turned the key over and over, examining it from every angle. "I can't even place what culture might have crafted it." Focusing his attention on the metal looping pattern, he wondered aloud, "I mean, I don't think it's Celtic, but I can't say that with any certainty. And how did it end up out there on the beach? It's not like anyone would just drop such a treasure." Reluctantly pulling his gaze from the key, he set it on the table between them. He turned his attention to Evan, trying to convince him, "I'm sure there's tons we can learn from it. Just look at it. It must be hundreds of years old." Noting that Evan wasn't happy about handing over the key, he added, "Besides, what are you going to do with it?" This felt like a low blow to Evan as if wanting to keep the key was just a silly, childish idea.

"Fine," Evan mumbled as he shoved the key towards his parents. He got up from the table, leaving his half-eaten fish sandwich and basket of fries. He wasn't hungry any longer. As he walked past the old sea captain character on his way out of the restaurant, the man's gaze did not follow Evan but remained fixed on the key still laying before his parents on the table. He felt a strange chill run through him, which quickly burned off when he heard his mother say from behind, "Honey, we'll see you back at the room. Remember we are getting up early tomorrow for a family expedition. Don't stay out too late." Evan wanted to become invisible at that very moment. He couldn't exit the restaurant fast enough. "Love you," she called as an after-effect across the crowded room, causing Evan to cringe even more. How could he have come from these people, he wondered as he stomped into the humid night air? Another log was placed on his bonfire of rage.

The restaurant was located next to a marina, and he paced along the maze of docks after storming out. He had nowhere to go but refused to return to their hotel room until he was sure his family had gone to sleep for the night. He didn't want to talk to any of them, even if only two of them would have talked to him in return. Like a monk in a labyrinth, Evan tried to focus his mind on the present act of walking, hoping to cool his burning temper. But the exercise only seemed to ratchet his heat further. His fists remained clenched, his rapid breathing persisted, and his jaw stayed locked tight, as he stamped against the wooden planks. He sat down at the end of the dock and kicked at the black water below, but the water was too far away, and his foot was met with only air. He growled at nothing and no one.

Wanting to calm down, he tried to picture himself like a viewer from the outside. It was a technique his dad had once suggested he use to help after an outburst. It had worked a few times, so why not try now? Starting at the top, he pictured his wavy dark blonde hair, unruly like his emotions. He rolled his eyes at the comparison. He looked down at the olive skin on his arms. It appeared darker than usual, perhaps from spending the day in the sun or maybe from the shadow of night. At the edge of the dock, he placed his hands on either side of his slim hips stretching out his long legs and tensed the muscles of his thighs and calves. He was pleased that his lanky limbs were beginning to take on more shape and that dark hair had begun to sprout and curl. He then bent his left elbow and flexed his tightened fist, causing his biceps and forearm to contract and enlarge. Not bad, he thought but vowed to spend more time doing daily calisthenics like his brother. He could stand to be a bit bulkier. He noticed his heart rate and breathing had begun to slow. The practice had worked.

His mind was quieter now, and he was able to hear the ambient sounds of the marina. The way rocking could calm a crying baby, the syncopated clinks of the lines striking the masts of the boats that bobbed on the gently undulating water soothed the last remaining bits of Evan's fury.

It was a dark night with clouds covering the moon and stars. He could see a few lights from boats further out in the calm waters of the Gulf, but the buildings behind him were all dark. He felt as if he was the only one still awake. No fish were jumping. No insects were buzzing or crawling past. The birds had long since settled in their roosts. Even the wind was done for the day. Everything felt still, including his previous torrent of emotions.

He gazed past his feet to the ink black water a few inches below and saw small swirls of bioluminescent light blooming up from the depths. Evan had always been fascinated by how various organisms, like fireflies and some fish, could produce and emit light. He had read that even damp wood may sometimes glow in the dark woods at night. While he had never personally witnessed the phenomenon, he hoped he might someday. As he watched the process unfold before him in the dark water, he tried to recall the science behind it. He knew there was something about a bioluminescent organism that would chemically react to oxygen, but he was never good with those kinds of details. Evan knew that if Ross were here beside him now, and still talking, he would remember that chemical's name and all of the details. Ross the walking encyclopedia... the now silent encyclopedia. Evan felt another pang of loss for his former brother.

The whirling clouds of light in the inky water below him appeared to be coming from almost-invisible, clear worms, no bigger than a staple. The puff of light seemed to propel the creatures through the water in a non-direct path, their minuscule bodies unable to control the thrust, causing them to spiral out of control. He counted the space between the bursts and realized the glow erupted every thirty seconds. Like an orchestrated fireworks show, these tiny beings flashed and twirled for several minutes below Evan. He recalled reading that bioluminescence may be the most common form of communication on Earth. He wondered what these little creatures were saying.

After meditating on the glowing water, the squall that had raged inside him early was only a distant memory on the horizon. He felt spent, exhausted by the force of his emotions. Like so many times before, after being unable to contain his eruption of feelings, he felt a heavy sadness. He was sad he had stormed away from his family. He knew they were on his side and loved him, which only made him feel more ashamed. Intellectually, he also knew they were right about the key, but that didn't ease the dull ache that throbbed at the thought of having to surrender it. He actually missed it, this object he only held for an afternoon. He couldn't help but feel like the key had come to him, that he was supposed to find it and discover what secrets it kept. He knew the key was lost to him now though, and he resigned himself to this defeat as he yawned.

Like banking a campfire, he tucked away the heat of his ire and yielded to his exhaustion. Spending most of his day in the sun and in a state of anger had worn him out completely. He returned to the hotel room with no urgency to his pace. It was well after midnight, and he found his family already asleep. He quietly brushed his teeth in the dark of the small bathroom. Without changing out of his swim trunks, he slipped under the covers, careful not to disturb his brother in the bed beside him. As he turned on his side, ready for sleep to take him, he felt Ross' hand give an awkward pat on his shoulder. Without saying anything, his touch communicated that he understood Evan's disappointment and that he too was sorry the key was gone.

Chapter 3

"I'm really looking forward to today, boys," their dad said as he flung open the hotel curtains, allowing the morning light to flood the room. Ross sat up quickly, ran through a quick sun salutation, as was his daily ritual, and then went off to the bathroom to get ready. Evan moaned, instantly annoyed by his brother's discipline and his lack thereof. He was already abandoning his pledge from last night to exercise more. He pulled his pillow over his head to block out the offensive glare. He felt the heat of his anger rise again. It was as if the sunlight coming into the room was the spark needed to reignite the smoldering coal within him.

"Oh, Evan. We are going to have a blast. We have the kayaks reserved for the entire day, the cooler is packed with sandwiches and drinks, and your Dad and I promise not to talk about work." His mom winked and smiled at his dad, who mirrored the same in response. "It's going to be a good day. Please just choose to be happy," his mom pleaded, repeating a phrase she often said. As if it was that simple. Evan resented the implication that if he just chose happiness, then all of his problems, including having a silent brother without any friends, would resolve. Choosing happiness wouldn't return the key to him.

"Fine, Mom, this is me choosing happiness," Evan said with a sharp slice of sarcasm and roll of the eyes. As he rose from the bed, he pasted a fake smile to his face. He slipped on his t-shirt and flip-flops and walked out the door. "I'll wait for you guys down by the water," he said before the door slammed shut behind him. He knew he had no plans to choose happiness and had instead decided to make the day miserable so that everyone knew where he stood on the matter.

It wasn't long before his family arrived at the shore with the cooler and life-vests. No one spoke, as if they were all taking a turn at Ross' practice of silence. Evan refused to make eye contact and stared down at his feet. He kicked chunks of gravel towards the water, thinking it was going to be a long day.

However, once everything was loaded up and they were underway, Evan couldn't help but enjoy himself. He had always loved being out on the water. With each stroke of his paddle, he felt himself glide across the surface, racing further from the shore. He had the sensation of flying - his kayak, his wings, and the liquid below him, the air through which he soared. He paddled strong, leaving his family to follow behind. It felt good to be in the lead. He looked back at them, each with a broad smile, and he couldn't help but smile in return. He pulled his paddle stronger and faster, allowing his earlier frustrations to dissipate with hard work. This is where he was meant to be, surrounded by open blue-green water dotted with small green-brown islands. He felt free and safe here, in control of his boat and his emotions.

Ross eventually caught up with Evan and lifted his chin in the direction of a small island in the distance, off the port side of his kayak, indicating they should head that way. "Sure, why not. It will probably take a while to get there, but I'm up for it," Evan answered in reply. He was never one to turn down a challenge from his brother, and he paddled slightly harder on the right causing his boat to turn towards the target. Their parents shared a smile together, content to follow their sons' lead, relieved to see Evan's mood lift.

After another hour or so, the small island key grew in size and spread before them. It was larger than it had first appeared. The east side was an impenetrable mangal of mangroves reaching out into the sea like a web of fingers clawing outward to grab more space for themselves. Evan applauded this plant that could exist and even thrive where most could not, admiring how mangroves could drink the salty water and withstand the battering of violent storms and waves. Pulling the kayaks into the dense, intertwining branches of the mangroves to dock and explore would be too difficult, so they paddled around to the west side of the island. Evan was happy to find a patch of sandy beach.

The two brothers pulled their kayaks ashore and hopped onto the stable ground. Both reached their arms high and wide and arched backward. It felt good to stretch after several hours of paddling. Ross continued with his second full sun salutation of the day and was finishing up as their parents finally arrived. "This looks like a great place to picnic," their dad said, pulling his kayak to rest at the shoreline beside his sons' boats. "What do you think, Bret? Want to take a break here for a bite to eat?"

"Sounds lovely. You guys are hard to keep up with. I could definitely use a rest," their mom replied as she too stepped onto the beach, her breathing ragged with exertion. "This is a pretty big key. I had no idea there were islands this big set off from the main chain of the Keys. It would be fun to take some time to explore after we rest a bit. I'm starving. Let's have some lunch." His mother beamed in his direction as she wiped away sweat from her brow. "Nice pick, Evan."

"Ross pointed it out, but I'll take credit for it if it turns out to be cool," Evan teased, shoving Ross' shoulder in jest. Ross just smiled slightly in response, lifting his brow as if to say, "We'll see."

The family laid out a picnic of sandwiches, apples, bagged chips, and bottled water and then spent some time relaxing in the afternoon shade provided by the trees on the western side of the island, enjoying the open view of the expansive Gulf. They were in no hurry after their challenging morning paddle. Ross and Evan took a swim in the clear water while their parents sat in the shallows of the small, gradual beach watching their sons.

"Time is slippery, isn't it? I can't seem to hold on to a moment. They were just babies, and now they are practically grown. I feel like they will be men, gone from us the next time I look up," Evan could hear his mother say to his father as he walked back onto the island. He felt bad for being so angry with them before. They were good parents, great parents really, and he knew it. He liked spending time with his family, and he knew he was lucky for it. He just wished he could feel the same peace that his family seemed to channel with such ease.

"Alright, who's up for an adventure?" Evan asked with a playful tone as he slapped his hands together, rubbing them in anticipation. Despite his attitude at the outset, it had been a great day so far, and he was looking forward to spending more time together exploring the inner part of the island. The thick wall of trees seemed almost impenetrable, and he was looking forward to conquering the challenge. His family nodded in agreement and turned towards the trees, with Evan again in the lead. The tightly webbed branches of the mangroves created caves that blocked out the afternoon sun and lured him deeper into the center of the island. After only a few steps inside, Evan felt like he was no longer near the edge of the beach, but deep within a jungle that stretched for miles. The sound of water lapping onto the sand was replaced by the rustling of leaves and the calls of birds. Glimpses of feathers flashed higher up in the trees. Mosquitoes buzzed thickly around his ears.

Sticky wisps of spiderwebs clung to his face, and Evan quickly brushed them away, hoping any resident spiders were cast aside with them.

"Not too much further Evan, it's getting pretty buggy," his mom said as she slapped her cheek.

Evan slapped a giant, black and white striped mosquito that was piercing the skin of his left arm, leaving a bloody splatter on his hand, which he wiped on his trunks. "Ugh, you're right Mom. There are way too many bugs in here." And before he had even finished saying this, he saw and felt five more mosquitoes puncture his skin. It sounded like hundreds more were circling his head, preparing for an attack.

"Plus I think the clouds are getting a bit darker off to the west. We'll need to get going soon," his dad called from the back of the line that the family had formed.

"You're right dad. This just isn't worth going any further. The bugs are unbearable," Evan said as he turned around. The family headed back to the beach, but by the time they had packed their picnic supplies back onto the kayaks, the wind was whipping up white-caps on the water, and the sky was a dark slate with storm clouds standing tall and formidable against the horizon.

"This storm came up quickly. Even if we head out now, I doubt we'd be able to stay out ahead of it. I think we better sit this one out, Peter. I don't think it would be a very wise decision to be out on the water right now." His mom's face was tight with worry, and curls blew loose from her braid. "Hopefully it will pass just as fast as it blew in. What do you think, guys?" his mom asked, shifting her eyes quickly between her family and the sky.

His dad gritted his teeth in concern, also surveying the darkening sky. "It's getting late, though. I hate the idea of paddling back after dark. We didn't bring any lights for the kayaks." Evan realized his dad had a point after looking at his watch to see that it was already after four. The paddle over to the island had taken them over two hours this morning. If the storm lasted longer than thirty minutes, they probably wouldn't make it back before dark.

"We could just camp here for the night if we had to," Evan suggested. "We have some food and plenty of water left over. Let's wait out the storm and see." Evan noticed Ross perk at the mention of spending the night on this remote key. Ross couldn't resist an adventure.

Both parents retrieved their phones from their packs only to realize they had no signal. "Man, we can't even call to report where we are. I really hate the idea of keeping the kayaks overnight without permission," their dad said just as a strike of lightning sliced the sky followed by an immediate crack of thunder. "But I guess there are worse things than that. We're not going anywhere now, that's for sure."

The family hunkered down under the edge of the mangroves, which provided a surprising amount of cover from the storm that seemed to swallow up the island and the surrounding waters within only seconds. The blue-green shallows darkened to a cold steel grey. The few smaller islands, which previously had been visible in the distance, were now completely obscured by the rain streaming down. Large drops of water pelted the sand, leaving quarter-sized depressions, quickly making the once dry portion as soaked as the shoreline. The wind blew stronger, pushing the water into a frenzied churn, like the washing machine agitator working on the deep clean cycle. The Gulf seemed to swell, expanding beyond its normal volume, and the shoreline encroached on the island, shrinking its size in effect. Evan wondered if that was from the gallons of water spilling from the sky or surge of wind and pressure that accompanied storms. He also wondered where the birds were hiding. Were they huddled close together like his own family?

Lightning flashed all around them, causing Ross and Evan to pull closer to their parents. Evan tried to remember the last time his family sat this closely. As little boys, he and Ross would flank his father every night for story time. He would read with such gusto, mimicking the voices of each character, laughing with a too-big, too-deep voice or coaxing a sweet feminine whisper. Both boys would sit enthralled for hours resting their heads and hands on his broad chest, feeling safe, surrounded by his woody smell and warm, radiant heat. Evan then recalled sitting on his mom's lap while she would type, her arms reaching around him, working on an article for the magazine. She never seemed bothered by his heavy head leaning against her shoulder as she wrote. She would simply ask that he stay "quiet as a mouse." He also remembered waking to the cool light of dawn, piled in his parents' bed with Ross' arm draped across his belly, his mom's long dark hair tickling his neck and his dad's heavy, rhythmic breathing blowing across his forehead. The cozy smell of the soft cotton sheets surrounding them was a wonderful blend of both his parents, earthy and airy at the same time. He could never actually remember going to their bed in the night, or Ross climbing in to join them, but he loved being the only one awake in the early morning, while the rest slept for a few moments longer. All four of them, secure in the cramped queen-sized bed.

The four sat packed together now as the storm raged on. He caught a whiff of that same earthy, airy sent now, and it contrasted the metallic smell of the rain. Evan's legs were becoming stiff from being squeezed up close to his chest.

He had pulled himself into a tight ball, trying to keep dry, but the amount of water falling from the sky was like a pool being turned upside-down, and his attempt seemed futile. He straightened out his legs, allowing them to extend past the overhanging branches. They were completely drenched in seconds, but at least he could feel the circulation flowing in them again. He was surprised by how cold the rainwater felt, wondering how much less its temperature was than that of the air. He checked his watch. It was already twenty past five, and the storm wasn't letting up. It was hard to believe they had been waiting for so long already.

He looked over and noticed his parents engaging in a silent, knowing conversation about what to do next. There was still too much rain and lightning to even consider an attempt back to shore now. However, waiting any longer would definitely ensure they would have to kayak in the dark. They had a good idea for which direction the shore was, but none of them were confident enough to risk finding it in the cover of night, without lights.

That left spending the night on the island as their only option. They all had plenty of experience camping. Over the years, they had hiked the backcountry, sleeping without tents, collecting berries and edible, wild greens, catching fish and building fires with only a piece of flint and steel. Relatively speaking, sleeping on this island for the night would be fairly comfortable. If the rain passed, it wouldn't be too cold, and perhaps they would be able to catch a few fish before the sun went down. They had a few valuable supplies with them on the kayaks, since their dad always insisted on bringing what he jokingly called his "armageddon bag" with them on every adventure. He had compiled a survival pack of what he considered to be the basics: matches, fishing line and hooks, multi-tool and small first aid kit. At times like this, Evan was glad his dad had brought it along. They surely would need it.

The mosquitoes would probably be the biggest challenge tonight. He shuddered at the thought of the swarm that would likely descend upon them at sunset and sent up a wish to the heavy grey clouds for the rain to continue. He would prefer being wet to being the evening meal for thousands of hungry mosquitoes. Thinking of stinging insects reminded him of the time they accidentally disturbed a wasps' nest during a hike in an Amazon rainforest. While his stings numbered in the teens, poor Ross had received the worst of it and had to spend a few days in a small Brazilian hospital after receiving over a hundred stings, many on his face. Evan had been worried that his brother would never look the same again, but the swelling and discoloration eventually subsided, and Ross was back to himself after a week or so. Sitting so close to Ross now, he could see the faint purple outline of a few scars that had remained on his neck.

"It will only be for one night," his dad said, still looking at his mom. He squeezed her hand gently. She nodded in agreement, and it was decided without further discussion.

Evan felt a surge of excitement. He smiled, pleased that the simple day excursion had turned into something more thrilling. His frustration and anger that had boiled in him earlier in the day were replaced by the juiced anticipation at roughing it for the night on a key in the middle of the Gulf. Maybe this was paradise after all. He barely noticed the soaking rain that continued to fall, lost in his pleasure of the challenge before him.

<h1 align="center">Chapter 4</h1>

The deluge continued for only a short time longer, but a steady drizzle persisted through what would have been sunset had the clouds not blocked the retreating sun. Evan thanked the clouds for granting his wish, grateful that the mosquitos weren't too bad after all. Before total darkness set in, the family managed to catch three fish using a bit of the leftover sandwiches as bait. Ross surprisingly captured two mahi-mahi by climbing onto an outstretched mangrove limb and dangling his line into a cove. The bigger fish must have sheltered there during the storm, making them easy prey. Evan waded out a ways from shore to cast his line, but only had his bait stolen by fish stronger or smarter than him. Frustrated, he abandoned the impossible task of fishing and helped his dad collect loose branches from the edges of the mangroves to be used as firewood. Their mom stealthily snagged the other fish, a fair-sized mangrove snapper. She beamed with pride as she lifted the copper-speckled fish from the water. While starting the fire took some time after the dampening rain, their dad was able to get an adequate flame going, and by 8:00 p.m., they were feasting on grilled fish.

They stared into the glowing embers of their fire for several hours after dinner, telling stories. Their mom was even able to cajole Evan into singing a few folk songs with her; ones she used to sing to them as lullabies. The lingering mist of rain and excess smoke from the damp wood had the positive effect of keeping the mosquitoes at bay. It turned out to be one of the best nights they had spent together as a family for a long time. Enjoying the pleasure of the evening and each other, no one was in a hurry to retreat to sleep. However, they eventually ran out of easily accessible wood, and the warm glow of the fire was extinguished.

"I suppose we try and get some shut-eye," their mom said through a yawn.

The damp sand was not the most comfortable bed, but his family seemed able to acclimate and quickly drifted off to sleep, leaving Evan alone with his

23

thoughts. The clouds finally dissipated, and he laid on the cool sand looking up at the newly arriving stars. Bright moonlight washed the island and surrounding water in an ethereal blue, making it seem less like night but rather somewhat like being underwater. A symphony of sounds blossomed as the island came to life. He listened as the water lapped at the shoreline which set a rhythmic beat. Birds shook the remaining wetness from their feathers, and with each light, breezy gust of wind, drops fell from the branches and leaves, like little rain showers of their own, tapping out a counter tempo. Cicadas sang in a chorus of undulating vibrations.

Suddenly, the sound of footsteps made Evan sit erect and crane his neck towards the woods. The footsteps were not from something small, and his heart leaped. The hairs on his arm stiffened at the thought. Was it possible for anyone else to be on this island? He quickly took inventory of his sleeping family, making sure none of them had gotten up without him noticing. The three lay asleep on the sand beside him. His dad's left arm cradled his mom's head. Her dark curls spilt out onto the contrasting sand reminding him of tendrils of jellyfish he had seen washed ashore two days before. The crack of a branch breaking at the edge of the tree-line wrenched his senses back to the present. He looked again towards where he thought he heard more footsteps. An alligator? A big cat? He didn't think either was possible on a remote island like this, but his mind raced through the possibilities. It couldn't possibly be a bear, could it?

Rising to his hands and knees, Evan squinted, searching for movement in the tree-line. He debated if he needed to wake and alert his sleeping family. His head swung quickly back and forth as he craned his neck, straining to hear the smallest of sounds, searching for where the noise was coming. His movements suddenly froze when he saw a soft light peek from behind a twisted branch. He blinked and rubbed his eyes after seeing what he thought to be the contours of a human form that was strangely surrounded by an aura of soft blue light, deep in the mangroves. Keeping himself completely still, he kept his gaze fixed on the female outline that was gingerly stepping over tangled branches and ducking under low hanging limbs, making her way out from the dense growth of trees towards the beach where he now crouched transfixed. Was it the light from the moon that was reflecting off her whitest-blonde hair and pure pale skin, making both seem to glow an icy blue? It was as if she was made from the same stuff as the bioluminescent sea-worms that he had watched the night before. How could that be? When she reached the edge of the mangroves, she noticed Evan's intense stare and stiffened, fixing an equally concentrated gaze back upon him. Crystal blue eyes pierced through the darkness, freezing Evan to the core. Neither moved, breath suspended until the shuffle of a bird from deeper within the branches startled her, and she streaked away like a deer from a hunter, back into the dark depths of the island.

Evan shook off the shell of ice that had glassed over his mind like a spell. On instinct, he jumped to his feet and took off after her. Running through the mangroves at night was like trying to navigate through a tangle of bodies, each one grabbing out with restraining hands. The mangroves' knees tripped him, their arms knocked his head, and their fingers clawed and scratched his exposed skin. Again, he was wishing he had grabbed his sandals first before darting off on this chase, just like the day before when he had stormed out of the hotel and had stepped the key. He paused to search the trees surrounding him, panicked that he had lost track of her. Heaving ragged breaths, hunched forward with his hands on his upper thighs, he saw a flash of the girl's glowing pale hair in an opening of branches up ahead.

Again, without thinking, he pressed forward, deeper into the island's interior. He ran face first into a spider's web and stopped to frantically brush the sticky thread from his hair, forehead, cheeks, and neck. As he simultaneously checked for a startled spider and swung his head around desperately looking for her, he was shocked to find that he stood before the opening of a low, dark cave that reached into the ground.

Still wiping the sides of his face, he again searched for the mystery girl, but she was nowhere to be seen. The surrounding woods were completely dark and silent. She must have disappeared into the cave before him. This was crazy! He had never heard of caves in the Florida Keys. He knew there was a system of underwater caves, sinks, and springs, on the mainland which comprised the Florida aquifer, and he had read about caverns in the state's panhandle region while looking at a brochure about its state parks, but caves in the chain of islands which dotted the waters between the Gulf and Atlantic? No, it wasn't possible.

He tried to remember how caves formed. His mind quickly darted to information he had learned while at Mammoth Cave in Kentucky. That cave system had formed by water seeping through the limestone to create a karst topography which consisted of underground drainage systems with sinkholes and caves. How could caves form out here and if they did, wouldn't they just fill with sea water? The Keys were just small outcroppings formed by sands and crushed coral that had been deposited by tides on shallow reefs, filled in by vegetation that grew in the dirt fertilized by bird droppings. There were no caves here according to every map he had ever seen, but it had to be possible because directly before him was the opening to what was obviously a subterranean cave.

The impulses that had compelled him into the woods at night without pausing to think had now slowed. He began doubting any of this was real. He tried to convince himself he was actually sleeping beside his family on the beach and only dreaming of this mystery girl. He only had imagined a crazed chase through the mangroves at night, and this cave before him was only a delusion. The insect bites and scratches on his arms were only further hallucinations. Perhaps all the daydreaming he had concocted about his mystery key and the treasures it held, combined with his fatigue from the kayak trip, had fueled this nighttime fantasy. Dream or not, Evan didn't pause further to consider whether he should continue his pursuit. He ducked into the blackness of the cave. Not only did he need to figure out who this girl with glowing hair and skin could be, but he also had to know where this cave might lead.

The first tunnel was so low to the ground, he had to proceed on his hands and knees. The rough, brittle limestone ceiling of the tunnel scraped and crumbled against the shirt on his back. The floor was damp and spongy littered occasionally with hard debris that cracked and crumbled under his weight. He wished he could see through the hood of darkness to know what he was crawling over. The scene from Indiana Jones and the Temple of Doom came to mind - the one where Short Round and the female lead go into that underground palace tunnel in search of the missing Doctor Jones and find themselves in a room with thousands of bugs flanking the walls, ceiling, and floors. He swallowed hard and forced himself to move faster forward, refusing to think of those crunching "fortune cookies." He could feel the earth slant sharply downward, causing his hands and knees to slide at times, and he wondered how deep he would go.

He brushed aside the many dangerous possibilities that swirled in his mind, and it was then that it dawned on him that he had no way of knowing that the girl he was chasing had even entered this hole. He had only acted on a hunch. Perhaps she was just hiding somewhere in the dark woods on the surface. He realized how stupid this was. He knew better than to crawl into holes, much less alone, in the night and without a light. He could picture his parents disapprovingly shaking their head at his poor decision making, but he pressed forward just the same, like a magnet being pulled by a stronger force.

The deeper he pushed into the cave's depths, the more compelled he felt, convinced there was no way he could turn back now.

Evan thought his eyes were playing tricks on him when he saw a pale blue glow in the distance. Relieved that he had been correct to pursue her into the cave, he was confused by the light pulsing up ahead. Did she have some sort of flashlight with her? Was there an opening up beyond and was the bright moon casting its glow? But then he caught a glimpse of her, and he couldn't deny that light was indeed radiating from her.

His urgent pace slowed as the tunnel opened into a cathedral-like room before him. He extended his limbs, standing to his full height. After the long crouched passage through the tunnel, Evan paused to stretch and take in the scene before him. His breath caught in his throat, and he made an audible gasp. It was like he was standing in the doorway of an old train station, the room before him was so expansive and grand. Stalactites hung from the ceiling as drops of water dripped from their tips, falling to the reaching cones of rock below which stretched up to meet them. A large pool in the center of the room swirled with light, causing reflections to sway on the ceiling and walls, casting shadows that chased in the corners. The water was filled with millions of bioluminescent organisms, dancing like synchronized swimmers performing a choreographed routine in rhythm with a silent song. It was there at the edge of the water that the girl sat, arms wrapped tightly around her knees, her chest heaving as she tried to catch her breath. Her faint glow seemed to pulse slightly with each breath. Her eyes were fixed on Evan.

Surely he was dreaming. Before he knew it, he would wake with the sunrise on the beach, and his family would pack up for the paddle back to shore. Maybe the entire trip to the island was part of the dream, and he was still asleep in the hotel bed beside Ross. He didn't care if this was a dream or not, and was determined to enjoy this beautiful delusion before it ended.

Evan was afraid to move any closer for fear the girl would run off again, and he wanted to take all of her in before she did. Her long hair fell in waves over her shoulders and cascaded down the length of her back. It continued to radiate a soft blue light despite any possible reflection from the moon. He had initially thought it was a blonde, but it was so pale that it was almost white. Now, as he studied her, it seemed like each strand was clear, devoid of any color at all, and instead filled with some strange sort of glow, like fiber-optic strands. Her skin also seemed to lack any pigment and had a translucence that revealed a delicate web of veins below its cover. There also was an unexplainable luminosity to her, preventing her paleness from appearing corpse-like but rather appearing to burst with energy and life. Her eyes shimmered with an icy brightness. Evan estimated she was about his age. Her lean body was beginning to show the curves of a woman. He was struck by what she was wearing and congratulated himself for conjuring such an unearthly imagination in his dream. It appeared she was clothed in a slate grey, form-fitting skin, almost like a wetsuit, but it appeared softer and more supple in texture - almost as if it were a life-like part of her - a second skin. Her hands and feet appeared slightly larger than his, not freakishly so, with an elongated grace about them. She was barefoot like he was, and he wondered if her feet ached like his did after the chase through woods and crawl through the cave tunnels.

As her breathing slowed, the tempo of her pulsing glow slowed as well. Evan dared to take a step closer. To his surprise, she stood slowly and returned his advance with a step in his direction. She was tall, nearly his height, with long, firm muscles flanking her arms and legs. She looked like an Olympic swimmer with broad shoulders and a narrow waist. Her beauty was striking. Evan forced himself to swallow and keep his breathing slow. Like swings of a pendulum, they took turns inching towards one another until they were only an arm's distance apart. They both stood spellbound. It struck Evan that she was just as fascinated by him as he was by her, and he watched as her eyes darted from his hair to his shirt to his feet back to his eyes. She seemed to be taking him in frantically before she awoke from her dream too.

She was the first to make contact, stretching out her arm full length to touch him, checking to see if he were real. Her fingers landed lightly on his chest and jerked back as if she had been shocked. Evan's breath simultaneously jumped with surprise. After looking down at the tips of her fingers to see she was unharmed, she tentatively reached out again, this time with her touch grazing his cheek. She's so bold, he thought, surprised by how much he liked it. As her hand slowly pulled back from his face, it was then that Evan noticed the thin, almost clear skin that connected her fingers. Were her fingers webbed? He incredulously wondered what other oddities her beauty concealed.

Without his conscious consent, his hand lifted to meet hers, again as if drawn by some magnetic force stronger than his own will. His boldness scared and excited him. Her butter-soft skin was cold compared to his clammy touch. He took her hand in his to examine it. Turning it over, he confirmed the webbing of skin that stretched between her fingers, gently spreading each apart. Were her toes webbed as well? He couldn't help but wonder. She seemed equally enthralled by the space and separation between his fingers as she traced the peaks and valleys of each. She turned his hand over in hers, inspecting both sides. He had never held a girl's hand before and was stunned by the thrill it elicited in him. He suppressed a giggle but couldn't contain his smile.

Evan realized he hadn't been breathing and took in a quick breath, startling her. She pulled her hand back but didn't pull her body away. Drawn by an equally magnetic pull and undeterred by fear, her gaze now settled on his shirt. One brow raised with fascination and confusion, she again reached out, this time to stroke the cotton fabric. Her hand slid down the length of his arm, causing his hairs to buzz with electricity. His tanned skin again seemed even a deeper bronze in contrast to her paleness. Her touch then traced the fabric band of his wristwatch. Her fingertips encircled the softly glowing face which coincidentally emitted the same cool blue light as her skin and hair.

Evan couldn't resist being led by his own enchantment, and his hand floated up as if pulled by the strings of a puppeteer to stroke her faintly glowing hair. Closely examining the lock between his fingers, he was struck by its subtle phosphorescence, unable to comprehend its source of light. It was silky and cool. As it slipped easily around and through his fingers, it released a faint fresh, sweet smell, reminding him of spring water. He had never been this close to a woman, aside from his mom, of course. While he certainly had spent plenty of time imagining what it would be like, in no way could he ever have anticipated it to be like this. Conflicting emotions overwhelmed him. He felt strong and weak, excited and scared, bursting, and empty all at the same time. Every part of him seemed to hum, an unknown energy surging throughout.

As his fingers glided through her lock of hair, he noticed a strange device just above her left temple. A small clear disk, almost like a suction cup, clung to the side of her face on her temple at the hairline. In sync with her glow, it pulsed slowly, like a breath or a heartbeat. Like her, it glowed faintly and then a bit more brightly in undulating rhythm. He allowed his fingers to explore it and found it was cool and yielding, similar to a jellyfish in its consistency.

Their fingers continued to explore beyond their own will in a tactile dance of discovery until their gaze met, causing both their eyes and hands to fix together as time seemed to freeze. The lightness and clarity of hers searched the depths of his own dark brown eyes. Their hands paused in holding. Their breath aligned in rhythm. They stood bewitched. As he breathed in, her delicate smell filled his senses. It distinctly reminded him of the smell of the clay along the beach at Whidbey Island on the Puget Sound. It was a complex fragrance that was both earthy and marine-like and also intoxicating. Her smell! He was unable to recall a dream that had overwhelmed his senses as they were now, let alone one that ever contained a smell so unmistakable. He couldn't even remember dreaming in smell before now. This was next level incredible.

He stood transfixed, trying to make sense of this. He was astounded at how similar and different they were at the same time. They breathed in the same rhythm, blinked with the same regularity, were made from the same basic cells. They were roughly the same height, and she was shaped like an average teenage girl...well...above average, Evan had to admit. She was beautiful. She was human; he was sure of it, but it was as if she had formed in some parallel universe. She certainly was not from his world, and he was not from hers. What world had she come from then? Where had his dream taken him?

Chapter 5

Evan snapped back into sharp focus when her hand left his and removed the device from her temple. The gaping suction sound startled Evan, and he took a quick step back in surprise. He was shocked when she reached forward and brushed aside his curling hair and placed it like a suction cup on the left side of his head, just below the hairline. The instant the jelly-like glob engaged, Evan was flooded with a surge of images, a streaming slide-show flashing in his mind. He saw himself on the beach with his family beside him, the glowing moonlight surrounding them. Then, he saw flashes of dark branches rushing past as they had when he had chased her through the mangroves. Pictures of his shirt, hands, and face, being examined up close, ticked through his mind. The images continued in an unending flow like the current of a fast-moving river. He saw dark caverns, similar to the one in which they now stood and snippets of undersea footage, like scenes from a nature documentary. A vision of what looked like parents standing together, a mother with anger in her eyes and a father casting a pleading look. They had the same pale skin and glowing hair as the girl, the same intensity in their eyes. Were they her parents? Evan wondered. In response, he felt an affirmative sense pulse through him, like his mind nodded in confirmation.

His puzzling and overwhelming feelings grew when he realized that the images and thoughts were not his own. It was like his consciousness was being hijacked, overridden by an outside source. He blinked and shook his head in an attempt to clear his mind. What was happening? He couldn't understand or stop the streaming information. The pictures continued in flashes, like clips from a movie playing before his mind's eye. Groups of strangers, people who looked like her, dressed like her, standing in dimly lit rooms. Then a younger girl, a smaller version of her, lying in a bed flickered across the screen of his mind. The sensation of swimming, almost like a memory, filled Evan. His mind filled with images of swimming underwater with others swimming alongside. They were gliding with ease beside a whale. That couldn't be, could it? A whale?

Evan placed his hands on either side of his head, trying to still the storm of raging ideas. His breath was fast, his heart pounding. He lifted his face and found her gaze again. Those crystal blue eyes were imploring. A staggering clarity washed over him. The thoughts were from her. He was seeing her thoughts.

"Whoa, hold on now," Evan said as he tried to think amid the fury of images that had rushed through him. He ripped the gelatinous blob from his temple. His skin pulled like he was ripping off a bandage. And that's when it stopped. The torrent of pictures dried up like a faucet being turned off. The noise in his mind quieted. He looked at her quizzically and spoke, "But how? What's happening? Is this what this, this…" He struggled to find the right word. "Is that what this gadget is for? Am I seeing your thoughts? Are you using it to communicate with me? Are you hacking into my brain?" He held the object before her, accusation written across his face.

The girl stepped back in surprise and furrowed her brow with a skeptical look of confusion. "Nia, com nia sa doe la-ah," she said, shaking her head from side to side. More than speaking, it sounded to Evan like she was singing. Her words were soft and lyrical. Evan instantly realized that they clearly did not speak the same language, and her voice was like nothing he had ever heard. Her otherworldliness further confirmed. He felt his knees buckle, unable to support the gravity that was crushing down upon him. He slumped to the damp limestone floor, chalky bits of gravel pressing against the palm of the hand he used to support himself. He couldn't believe any of this could be real, so why did it feel so real, then? The blurred line between reality and fantasy scared him.

She bent before him and wrapped her cool hand around his. Gently, she led his hand back to the side of his face. A pleading look in her eyes implored him to place the device back onto his temple. He was sure he saw her emanating glow pulse softly as if she was trying to communicate something to him with her light. Unable to do anything other than comply, he stuck the jelly back onto his skin. His fingers against its outer surface felt the device throbbing to the beat of his racing heart. She kept her soft, cool hand atop his. Her touch had the effect of slowing the orb's pulse, and he felt his breathing slow to match its rhythm. Her other hand reached out to take his, and she pulled him back up to standing. She closed her eyes and breathed deeply, slowly. It was like she was filling herself up like a balloon, and Evan felt himself become lighter in response. His mind quieted. He felt more relaxed as his thoughts slowly returned to him. The swirling surge of images he had just experienced was replaced by a calm, meditative image of his family. He pictured them lying on the beach.

Rather than believing this was all a dream, he now hoped it actually wasn't real and tried to imagine himself lying beside his family asleep on the beach above. He closed his eyes and willed himself to wake up. He thought about returning the kayaks to the hotel tomorrow, his feet stepping into the ankle-deep water at the shoreline, the feel of the warm sun against his skin. As he did, the girl sucked in a deep breath and opened her eyes, causing him to respond in kind. She stared at him with a shocked, questioning look. Evan was overcome again. Could she see what he was thinking now?

Her head nodded in the affirmative. They were communicating without words by way of the device, which Evan assumed must be linking them somehow. Her hand was still touching his temple, so he seized the moment to run an experiment. He pictured his brother, taking time to capture all the details. He could see Ross' lanky frame, standing almost as tall as him now, both already taller than their parents. He visualized Ross' dark blonde hair, same in color to Evan's but much different in its orderly straightness and close cut. He allowed himself to remember Ross from earlier today, gesturing with his chin towards the island paddling the kayaks, a twinkle in his light green eyes. Then he paused, trying to clear his mind and allow her stream of images to return to him. As if in response, he again saw the younger girl who resembled the beautiful one standing before him appear on the screen of his mind. The girl in his mind had the same pale features and radiated the same cool glow. That was her sister, Evan guessed, and she again nodded in confirmation.

He tried another test to see if he was on to something. He thought of his mom and dad sitting across from him at the table last night, waiting for him to talk about his day. Like taking a photograph, he took time to document all their features. His mom's dark curls pulled free from her usual side braid that hung down over her left shoulder. His dad's perpetual five o'clock shadow with its rugged effect on his otherwise boyish flushed cheeks. Both seemed much younger than their actual ages, which were only betrayed by the deep creases around their eyes, caused by their frequent smiles. Picturing them like this inside his mind, Evan could see the joy and love that exuded from them both.

The next images that transferred to his thoughts were her mother and father - it had to be. The person standing before him now looked so much like the tall, icy woman that he pictured - this one only softer and gentler somehow. He was giddy with excitement. She continued to nod, more emphatically now, her eyes lighting up with validation that they were actually communicating. The woman she was describing for him was older but still strikingly beautiful. She stood beside a thin, taller man, who had chin-length wavy hair that also glowed with that unearthly cool light. They both had the same translucent skin and were wearing the same wetsuit-like outfits. Evan was struck by how regal they appeared. The woman stood with a rigid grace that commanded attention. The father, who stood a step behind, also had an air of authority but seemed to Evan to be less intense than the mother. So this is who she comes from, Evan thought, but where *does* she come from, he wondered further.

Evan didn't understand how it was possible, but in response to his questioning thoughts, he was presented with images that provided the answers. In his mind, he saw a system of caves that were lit much like the one in which they were standing now. Pools of water, some as small as bathroom sinks and some as big as Olympic swimming pools, were scattered throughout the caves. The pools were filled with the same bioluminescent swirling light, casting an alien lambency. Groups of people who resembled her, with the pale, luminous skin and hair, but in all manner of shapes and sizes, moved about with normalcy. All of the people wore similar attire, those elegant wetsuits, in varying muted shades of blue, grey, and green. Evan had a distinct understanding; this was the community to which she belonged. An urgency burned within him, like the grumble of a hungry belly. He wanted to see and know more.

Continuing the conversation - there was no other way to describe it - Evan conjured images of his world for her. He thought of Ross and him riding bikes in his grandparents' neighborhood. He saw her eyes flicker in fascination urging him on. He then tried to impress her by conveying some of his most memorable trips, remembering his favorite places from his family's travels. He thought of the bustling streets of Hong Kong that smelled like exhaust, cooking fish oil and flowers. Her eyes widened with shock, and she flinched. Desperate to soothe her, he recalled the quiet mountaintop in Peru where he felt like he could see forever. The fear melted from her expression, replaced by a reflection of beauty that washed over her face. He evoked the memory of an icy morning, freshly covered and muted by snow, like a marshmallow wonderland. Snow crunched and squeaked underneath his snowshoed feet as he hiked the dunes during a Michigan winter trip. Her eyes beamed in fascination. He felt a thrill swell up in him.

Wanting to share more of his happy memories, he thought of today, swimming with his brother in the clear water while his parents sat on the beach. Like being interrupted during any normal conversation, memories from her seeped in, as if she couldn't wait to say "No way! Me too!" and share her own common experiences.

Without even having to think about it, Evan paused his thoughts and allowed hers to continue, as if say, "No, please, you go ahead." Her memories began to stream, and she transferred scenes of swimming deep undersea. However, the image of swimming that she portrayed was very different from his own understanding. He could actually feel the pressure and weight of the water squeezing in. Groups of people, swimming together with purpose. It reminded Evan of the bustling streets of New York filled with morning commuters. Their swimming was experienced, driven by work, not playful like the swimming he and his brother did. Evan noticed they swam with a strange film over their noses and mouths. Like a camera zooming in with a tighter focus to answer the barrage of questions that were blooming in Evan's mind, he could see up close the apparatus pulsing with the swimmer's breath. It seemed to be made of the same jellyfish-like substance the communicator device he now wore on his temple was, and just like that, his quizzical thoughts were answered by her mind's display. She simply and succinctly described the instrument that worked like a respirator allowing them to breathe while swimming the long distances underwater. She nodded and smiled, confirming his understanding.

He applauded his ability to manifest such a marvelous dream. Feeling a sense of urgency, he worried he would wake at any minute. He wanted to soak it all in - the smell of her, the feel of her, the light spilling out of her, but then he had the crushing realization that the complexity of such an elaborate fantasy would actually be too sophisticated for him to conjure. The weight of it all bore down on him, and he felt sick. He could see the pain reflected in her face as well.

So if he wasn't dreaming, then what were the ramifications of this being reality? An underwater world? A whole group of glowing people who swam the ocean depths? Communication by way of a device that connects to your mind? If this was real and people like her actually exist, why had he never heard of it? Was he making a new discovery? Was she making the same but converse discovery by finding him? His mind was racing trying to figure out what came next. Who could he talk to about this? He was overcome by an overwhelming dread that if his parents found out about this, about her, it would all be taken away, just like the key.

"The key?" Evan felt the girl say as her body went stiff. Her hands gripped his more tightly, and her eyes bore into his as she demanded to know. "Where is the key?"

Evan blinked, even further confused. He couldn't understand how the images they had just been clumsily transmitting could now have morphed into what seemed like actual words. Not just words - she had a voice, and he could hear it inside his mind. It was the same lyrical voice as before, only now she was speaking in a language he could understand. She was coming in loud and clear in his language as if they had found the correct radio signal on the dial. If he needed more than that to try to figure out, it just dawned on him that he was the only one wearing the device. So how could any of this work? He felt lightheaded. Again without his permission or instruction, his body slumped to the ground, breaking the physical link they had been sharing. His mind cleared. He sat with his head leaning on his forearms, propped on his bent knees. She squatted before him, returning a hand to his temple. "Where is the key?" he heard her demand again.

Chapter 6

"What? I... I... I don't get it," Evan spoke the words out loud. He grasped at his thoughts, trying to make sense of what was happening, but like trying to hold water, all explanation and reason were spilling from his grip. He couldn't wrap his mind around any of this. "How can you hear my thoughts? How can I hear yours?"

She sat down in front of him and placed her hand on his knee. Without moving her mouth or saying a word, she responded. "The device. It transmits and receives ideas to streamline communication." She pushed again, "The key... do you know where the key is?" Her pleading eyes boring into his.

Unable to process what was happening, Evan was also unable to give any attention to her question about the key. He was consumed with trying to figure out how it was that he could hear her inside his mind, in his own language. Her simple explanation about the orb that pulsed at his temple didn't make sense to him. Why was it now conveying words instead of streaming images as it just had before? Why wasn't she as shocked and confused as he was? This was all way too crazy, moving way too fast. Desperate to make sense of things, he continued by asking, "Yeah, but you're not wearing one now, so how can you hear my thoughts? Plus, we don't even speak the same language... how can we understand each other's words?" Regardless of how elaborate, he was convinced that this had to be a dream.

"I'm female," she said curtly, shaking her head with impatience, as if, of course, all of this was so simple and perfectly clear. "Communication comes more naturally to us. Plus, I have the gift." Again her voice appeared within his thoughts even though she didn't speak the words aloud. Evan was shocked that not only he could hear her thoughts but sense her tone as well. He could hear the annoyance in her words in addition to seeing it plainly displayed on her face. Wishing to understand and appease her irritation with him, he conceded that women always did seem to have the upper hand when it came to communication. He thought of discussions between his parents and admitted that his mom was normally two steps ahead of his dad and seemed to know what he was thinking even before he did.

Just the week before, when packing for their trip to the keys, his dad had come into the living room carrying his open camera bag. Before he could even ask, his mom had told him that his extra set of lens filters were with his battery backup on the top shelf of the closet. His dad had smiled, winked at his wife before leaning in to place an affectionate kiss on her cheek. "Thanks, love. It's like you know what I need even before I do. What would I do without you?"

"Perish," his mom had jested, popping her hand against his dad's retreating backside in response, before resuming her own packing.

This skill his mom possessed had always intrigued and baffled Evan. She nodded to confirm that he was beginning to understand. She had seen his memory. Evan shuddered, taken aback by her presence inside his mind. His upper teeth pressed into his lower lip in concern. He was bewildered by how such clear communication could actually take place within their minds, but he was willing to concede that it was happening.

"Ok, I get it, we can communicate without talking." He paused to laugh at himself for unnecessarily saying the words out loud, and she also smiled. He continued by thinking the next sentence in his mind. "But I don't understand how it works." Evan searched her eyes for answers. He had recently read an article describing a new invention, a device like a hearing aid that could translate languages in real time conversation. It had sounded like science fiction to him, but he didn't question how it worked. He just trusted it was technology that worked. He felt himself begin to concede his doubts about the suction cup that was stuck to his temple, thinking that perhaps it operated similarly to the device he had read about in the article. The fact that it worked without words, transmitting direct thoughts instead, was a stumbling block to his full acceptance. If it instead operated like the new hearing aid, and he was hearing her lyrical words translated into his own language, that might be something he could comprehend. Having her thoughts simply stream into his own? That mystified and unnerved him.

"It's technology. It just works." She exhaled with a thrust of frustration, and her shoulders sagged. "I... I... I don't know how exactly," her thoughts stammered. "I don't work at the tech labs designing and building these things. We've just always had them or some version of them as long as I can remember. They help us communicate without words while we're out swimming. It's impossible to talk with our breathing masks in place, so we wear the transmitters. I don't know how it's translating our languages. It just must be built with that capability." She seemed flustered, trying to explain something that was obviously beyond her understanding. "We all have them, and they just work." She shook her head, pulled her lips into a tight line, and shrugged her shoulders in dismissal. "I don't know how to explain it better than that. It just works," she repeated. Her words flowed perfectly through Evan's mind along with her tone of impatience over his disbelief and her frustration to describe it any better.

Evan thought of his computer, tablet, and phone. If asked why any of those devices worked, he would be hard pressed to explain it also. He couldn't recall the first time he swiped his finger across the glass screen, and an application responded. They simply had always worked that way, as long as he could remember. He wouldn't be able to explain the engineering or science behind it if someone asked him. Even the watch on his wrist, with its GPS capability, was somewhat of a mystery to Evan. He knew it communicated with satellites in space and that somehow correlated his location on the planet, but if asked why the technology worked, he would shrug his shoulders and answer, "it just does." He was beginning to take her word for it, and she nodded, obviously pleased that he was catching up.

"So if I take this off," Evan asked, touching the pulsing jelly on his temple, "I won't be able to understand you?" His eyes searched hers for an explanation, and he was again struck by her overwhelming beauty. Evan struggled to swallow, finding his mouth and throat incredibly dry, and then had to remind himself to breathe. No girl had ever made him feel like this before.

She looked down, away from him, as if embarrassed. "Well, some have the gift, like me." She looked back up at him, and seeing the confusion on his face added, "the ability to hear it all, with or without the device. I'm still working on my technique and find I often have to be in contact with the person for me to hear them or transmit my own thoughts. Some I can hear without touching, though." Her soft fingers tightened on his hand at the word and the jolt of energy coursed through him again. Her lips upturned at the corners, obviously pleased with her effect. "Others have the gift too, mostly women, but a few men can communicate without the device."

She paused for a moment, turned her face from him, her eyebrows knitting, clearly thinking, as if trying to arrange her own thoughts. However, Evan heard and saw nothing transmitting through his mind. He wondered why he couldn't hear or see these thoughts of hers. How was she keeping them private from him? Were any of his thoughts secret, or could she hear all of his streaming questions? Evan suddenly felt very self-conscious. Had she heard him just now thinking about how beautiful she is? Did she know how she made him feel?

"Yeah... I can hear all your thoughts," she offered softly in reply. She spared him by not turning to look him in the eye. Evan blushed and felt heat course through him like a punch of lightning. Part of him wanted to run away and hide his emotions from her. It was mortifying to be so exposed. A girl at a coffee shop in Helsinki had once caught him looking at her from across the room, and he had become so flushed, he had excused himself to the restroom. His mom had called after him as he was walking away "But you just went! Is your tummy upset?" He saw the beautiful girl cover her laugh as she looked down into her coffee cup. He had wanted to implode there on the spot from the embarrassment of it all, but here with her now, his desire to run and hide was trumped by the magnetic force she exerted upon him and his urgency to understand if it was all actually real.

"Well, why can't I hear all of yours then?"

Her gaze then lifted to meet his, her cheeks flushed as well. "Please give me a moment. All your questions, your thoughts... this is all so overwhelming."

She stood and stepped back, releasing their contact. She placed her hands on her temples, closing her eyes as if trying to clear her thoughts and center herself. Even though he desperately wanted to keep his mind blank, embarrassed by what he was thinking, Evan couldn't help but be captivated by her. Her slender body turned slightly away from him, curved in all the right places. Her high cheekbones sloped into an angled chin that led into a long graceful neck. Her waving, glowing hair fell down over her strong shoulders and slender arms.

Worried that she could not only feel his burning gaze but hear his lustful thoughts as well, he forced himself to look down at the damp limestone ground. He picked up a handful of coarse dirt and tried to focus his attention on his fist as he let the bits stream from it to his other hand below. He then tilted that hand and felt the fine gravel sieve through his fingers, listening to the light patter as each grain fell to the ground. He repeated the process of scooping another handful and then allowing it to slip between his hands, trying to clear his mind with this hourglass effect. However, his mediation was only temporary, and the questions flooded back to him. He felt like he was drowning in the unexplained. Was he really dreaming? Was this actually real? How was her hair glowing? What about the webbing between her fingers? Did she live down here? Had she ever met anyone like him before? What did she know about the key?

Her eyes popped open, and in one step, she was in front of him again, crouched with her hand again to his temple. "The key? Where is it? I have to return it, or my parents are going to kill me!" She had a pleading, desperate expression on her face. Evan was afraid she might start crying.

"My... my parents took it," he stammered. "They want to have someone study it," he offered in weak explanation. "What do you mean your parents are going to kill you? Is it theirs?" Evan asked, trying to understand how she could possibly be connected to the enigmatic key he had found the day before.

"Oh, *goddess* no. It's not theirs...it's everyone's." She could read the confused look on Evan's face, and before he even had a chance to think his question, she answered, "it's the sacred key. I took it from the altar in the temple after a fight with my mom. My mother is sworn to protect it, and no one is supposed to touch it," she turned her head to the side, shame dimming the light of her face. She swallowed and continued. "Protecting the key...it's one of my mom's functions as matriarch. To get back at her during an argument, I took it." Emboldened by her confession, she returned to face him, took a deep breath, and went on. "In a rage, I ran away from home with the key and kept running past the tunnels that are off limits. I ran for hours, not paying any attention to where I was going and became lost." She paused again, obviously ashamed by exposing her weakness.

Evan reached forward, empathy compelling him, and held her hand in his. "I get it." He truly did. He knew too well how it felt to be lost in a flood of emotions, carried away on surging rapids, and he felt a bit of satisfaction knowing that he wasn't the only one controlled by anger at times. He nodded, urging her to continue, feeling her soften a bit with relief.

"I had never been so far from home, and I started becoming frantic. I wasn't paying attention to the turns I was taking. The more lost I became, the more distraught I felt. I pushed on for several more hours, desperate to find my way out from the dark maze of tunnels. I saw a light in the distance, so I ran towards it. I found myself at an opening. It felt so strange. The air had changed, it was hotter and thicker somehow, with a heaviness to it." Humidity, Evan could feel the damp Florida heat now, as if he were there in her memory with her. "And there was the light... it was so bright, I could barely see. I felt like I had gone blind." Her eyes squinted just from the memory of it.

Evan was reminded of coming out of a movie theater on a summer afternoon, assaulted by the heat of the day and temporarily blinded by the light after hours of cool darkness. "And it was so hot, searing my skin and burning my lungs as I breathed in." She scrunched her shoulders as she remembered the painful sensation.

After shaking the memory from her head, she fixed her eyes directly on his. Her expression was full of shock. "I couldn't believe it. I had actually come to the surface. I mean, I've heard the stories about the surface from my grandmothers and the other sibyls. Stories about the landmen and all the dangers the surface holds. But I thought those were just fables we were told as children to warn us against going off too far during a swim or wandering the tunnels by ourselves. I hadn't actually thought the surface was real and certainly didn't think there could possibly be any landmen...like you." She paused as if not believing her own words.

"Wait," Evan hesitated, stumbling over the concept. "Landmen? I'm a landmen or landman or landboy or whatever? And the surface? You mean... like the land? You've really never been to the surface before? So what you're saying is that you live underground... or underwater rather? Does that make you... a mermaid?" Like the last pieces of a puzzle which quickly fall into place, Evan was beginning to assemble all of the information that had eluded him before. He held up her hand and examined the interconnection of silky skin between her fingers. The translucent flesh that was thinner than paper showed a network of filigree veins. Likewise, with the same dubious fascination, she paused to marvel at his webless hands in response, nodding but then shaking her head.

"A mermaid? What? No, I'm... oh, my. Is that what we are to you?" she almost giggled as she too was putting it all together. It took Evan a bit longer for all the pieces to fit, but then he too couldn't help but smile at the paradox. He was a fable in her world like she was in his. Then the weight of it really struck him. If she was touching what she considered to be a "landman," then he must be touching a "mermaid." A choked laugh burst from him. He was touching a mermaid! This had to be a dream. No other explanation was possible. Mermaids aren't real, and he knew it. This was the longest and most real dream of his life. It was so fascinating. He had so many questions.

"You mean to tell me you have tales about landmen like our tales of mermaids? Like Ariel and The Sirens in Homer's <u>Odyssey</u>?" Evan asked.

Her eyes narrowed in skepticism, but her mouth broadened in a smile. "I don't know about any Ariel or sirens, but I do know this is just the craziest thing ever!" she replied. She couldn't help but laugh and shake her head dubiously. Summing it up perfectly, she added, "it's like we're living in parallel worlds, telling stories of each other's existence, but without knowing anything at all!"

"I know. Insane!" was all Evan could think to add in his state of complete befuddlement. He was still pretty sure that this was a dream and was unable to trust that any of this was actually happening. He laughed in response to her lyrical giggle that sounded like joyful notes popping from bubbles. Her beauty was magnified when she smiled. Her eyes brightened and sparkled. Her full lips spread to the widest, most lovely smile Evan had ever seen, and with that, her hair glimmered more brightly.

Suddenly conscious that she could read his admiring thoughts, he tried to mentally change the subject. "I wonder if we are the first to ever meet? Do you think this is the first mermaid/landman encounter? Or do you think others have met in the past, but no one ever believed them? Maybe that's where our myths and legends about each other come from. I mean, if I told anyone about this, they would think I was crazy for sure." He tried to imagine how Ross would react if he told him about this encounter. He cracked a laugh when he thought about it. "That might make him talk again!"

She joined him again in nervous laughter. "Yeah, my sister would never believe this... none of this. A landman, ha! I mean, seriously, who would ever believe it?" Her face stiffened. "I'm still not even sure I do. I keep waiting to wake up from a dream." She shuddered visibly, and worry returned to her face. " I sure hope I wake up soon. I just wish this was all over."

Evan couldn't hide his hurt, so she rushed to explain. "No, not because of you." Her face warmed with a smile, and she lightly stroked the skin on his hand, causing Evan to swoon. It was the best sensation he had ever felt. He could barely focus as she continued to clarify. "I just wish I could wake up at home before any of this mess started. Before I stole the key. Before I ran away. Before I got lost. When I made it to the surface, I was totally stunned. By the time my eyes finally adjusted and were able to to see through all of the light, I stumbled over the hard, rope-like tangles, tripping and falling with almost every step." The mangroves, Evan thought. She nodded, glad of his understanding. "After some effort, I made it through and found I was alone on a small bit of land surrounded by water." She paused as if trying to find the right word to describe something with which she was so unfamiliar.

"You mean the island, right?" Evan offered.

"Yes, an island, the very same place I found you tonight. When I stepped from the shade out into the intense light, my skin…" She paused to grimace. "I felt like it was on fire. The air was so very hot. I couldn't breathe. I was so disoriented. When I rubbed my eyes, trying to adjust, I dropped the key." She shook her head at the memory with a look of disappointment on her face. "I'm still not quite sure how it happened, but as I was bending to pick it up, a bird swooped down and snatched up the key. A bird! I had heard about them in the landmen lore, but to actually see one, and watch it fly away with the key, it was magnificent and horrible at the same time! Like that," she startled Evan by snapping her fingers, "the key was gone." She pressed her hand across her brow and looked as if she might cry. "If I don't get it back and my mom finds out…" she swallowed hard. "If anyone finds out, I'm… I'm… Oh goddess, what have I done?" She shook her head, closed her eyes, and turned her face downward.

Evan could feel her agony in the pit of his stomach. He knew that feeling that plagued him after committing a wrong. He felt it often after losing his temper and flying off the handle at his family. He gently placed his hand under her chin, lifting her gaze to return to his. "I don't understand much of what's going on, and I'm not sure how, but I will help you get the key back. I promise."

Chapter 7

The gravity of the situation pressed upon Evan, and he felt very tired. He tried to replay the night's events in his mind in order to convince himself he must be dreaming since that seemed to be the only plausible explanation for how he had come to be standing in an underwater cavern holding hands with a beautiful mermaid. What else could he call her - this mysterious girl who needed his help to find an even more mysterious sacred key. But the intensity of her pleading eyes, locked with his, the grip of her hand, sending jolts of energy through his palm with each heartbeat, the presence of her, standing before him and possessing his thoughts, it was all so real. Never before had he conjured a dream this vivid and complete. Never before had he felt tired while dreaming - could you even be tired while sleeping? Despite the exhaustion that draped over him like a lead blanket, he had never felt more alive. Was this all real?

The pain on her face certainly looked real, and its effect on Evan felt real too. Driven by his desire to help, he took a deep breath, filling himself with confidence. He nodded to convince her, as well as himself, that he could do it. Buoyed by the effort, he thought it seemed easy enough. He simply had to go get the key and bring it back to... his thoughts stumbled, "But I don't even know your name."

She smiled. "Maera." She said it aloud, rolling the "r" slightly. He loved the look of her lips and tongue as she said it. It sounded like a song dancing through his mind as he repeated it over and over. It didn't have the same lyrical quality when he heard himself say it though. She giggled at him, and he was embarrassed, again forgetting she could hear all his thoughts. He felt so exposed to her like his mind was naked, but instead of feeling violated or threatened by his vulnerability, he felt safe with her.

"I'm Evan. Evan Newman." Out of habit, he said this aloud, cringing as his voice sounded so flat and hard to him.

"Well, Evan, Evan Newman, it's nice to meet you." Her eyes twinkled at him, but he didn't notice her ribbing.

Fumbling in response, "No, it's just Evan," he corrected her gently. "Newman's my last name. We landmen have two names, one that's our own, and the other that belongs to our family group," he awkwardly rambled, instantly feeling ridiculous by using the term landmen to describe himself.

Again she giggled, shaking her head. "I figured. I was just teasing you." Evan blushed again realizing how silly he must sound to her. He wondered when he would get used to her always having the upper hand, able to hear his thoughts. Trying to soothe his bruised ego, she added, "we also have two names. Mine is Maera, Maera Melusina." She laughed at her own joke, and it sounded like notes from a magical instrument. He couldn't help but laugh as well.

"Beautiful and funny." Evan was shocked at how bold he was with her. He hadn't had much experience around girls his own age, spending most of his time only with Ross and his parents. The few times he had been around them though, he was shy, allowing his brother to do most of the talking. Well, that is before Ross had stopped talking. He certainly never had flirted so openly with one before now. He supposed his assertiveness had something to do with the fact she knew what he was thinking anyway. He figured there was no way of hiding his attraction to her. "Don't tell me you're smart, also."

She lifted an eyebrow and the corner of her mouth in a sly smirk. "I guess you'll have to wait and see."

Evan flushed at the realization that she was flirting back with him. Afraid of where his racing mind might lead, he quickly changed the subject. "Ok then," he cleared his throat to steer the conversation away from his attraction to her. "Let's formulate a plan to get that key back."

Her relaxed expression stiffened as dread returned. She wrinkled her forehead with worry. "I can't go home without it. I'm already going to be in so much trouble for taking it... for even touching it." She closed her eyes in torment.

Evan remembered the beautiful key, its otherworldliness. He was proud of his intuition for knowing it was something of great importance, but couldn't understand how it could be such a source of agony to her. "Why is it so special?" he asked gently. He rubbed his thumb gently across the silky skin on the back of her hand, coaxing her eyes open.

She exhaled deeply before explaining. "It's the sacred key. It's our people's most protected and important treasure, central to our belief system." She chuckled at the coincidence, puzzling Evan, but quickly explained. "It's actually connected to our myth about landmen." She paused, and Evan could feel her arranging her thoughts before she proceeded.

"The story my grandmother tells, goes like this. Years and years ago, we were all one people, the Meram and the landmen. That's what we call ourselves, Meram." She checked to see if he was following before continuing, and Evan nodded. "We all lived together on the surface as a single tribe. One day, the earth violently shook and split her seams, opening a deep trench. Half the tribe, most of them women, fell deep into the earth, so deep that they couldn't escape. The fallen people banded together, intent on surviving and forged a new way of life in the caverns under the sea." She gestured with her hand to the room around them. Evan continued nodding as he looked around the vast cathedral of a room, trying to imagine what life down here might be like. A damp chill slipped down his arms.

Maera continued. "The ancients developed strong communities, led by strong women. They adapted and flourished in this undersea world, living closely with the ocean. They thrived by aqua-farming, producing food and clothing from the plants and animals swimming in the waters around them. They learned to cultivate bioluminescent organisms, lighting their homes with glowing pools of light. As you can see, we have even come to adorn ourselves with the light," she added, casting her gaze towards a tress of hair which spread across her shoulder. It continued to emit the softest radiance. Evan couldn't resist and indulged to stroke a strand of her glowing tresses. He was beguiled by how it was able to be both clear and multicolored at the same time, an elusive iridescent rainbow. When he reached its end, he twirled the lock around his middle finger with his thumb, marveling at the strands of light. She smiled and continued.

"We developed the ability to harness geothermal energy and have made many technological advances." Her eyes motioned to the orb on Evan's temple. "But through our evolution, we maintained a connection to our primitive ancestors and kept the story of the surface alive through our worship. For generations, our people searched for the opening to the surface, confident that they could reunite with the lost tribe of landmen, but no one ever found it. Or so they say..." she pulled her lips tight and raised her eyebrows in a look of mistrust. "After a time, the idea of the surface changed from being an actual place to more of an idea, a symbol. Most people now don't even believe it exists or ever did, but that the surface is a sort of fable, created to give our lives meaning and purpose. The surface represents another part of ourselves, a part that has become locked to us. Only the sacred key, made in meditation by our foremothers years ago, is capable of unlocking that part of ourselves. The key became our central symbol and is revered and praised for being 'the way' to our whole selves, something to which we are supposed to aspire." She rolled her eyes at this last bit.

Evan thought of the towering cathedrals in Europe and layered pagodas in Asia that his family had visited. He recalled how they were filled with mystic symbols and valuable artifacts, serving as places of worship for the devoted who searched for a connection to God or Heaven or salvation. While he had accepted the concept of faith in the abstract, academic way in which his parents had described it, he never had a personal connection with the divine. He never felt the desire to have one. He understood how people felt drawn to the symbols of their faith and honored their importance with art and jewelry, like wearing a cross necklace, for instance. However, he had never felt an attachment to any of the symbols or meanings. Because of this, he thought he understood her agnosticism. "So you don't believe any of this, do you?" he asked.

"It's not a matter of believing. I've heard this story my entire life. My mother, the matriarch of our people, is charged with the key's safe keeping. She has devoted her entire life to it. Sometimes, I think she loves the key more than she loves me. It's like an obsession our people have... they worship the key in a desire to be whole." Maera exhaled deeply and then chewed at the inside of her cheek as if she was searching for a way to explain. "I just don't buy it. I don't understand why aren't we good enough the way we are. I mean, I feel complete as I am. I don't have the feeling that something is profoundly missing, and because of this, I feel so different from everyone else. They all seem to get it... the key, the mythical surface, the quest to be made whole. They worship the key and all it represents. Some spend hours in meditation seeking 'the way.' People make pilgrimages to the key, and my mom, asking for her guidance. It's her job to lead people on that quest, and she spends her days studying and giving lectures on this stuff."

Evan imagined her mother being like the Pope or the Dalai Lama. He pictured the flocks of people who seek out her wisdom. Maera understood his thoughts instantly, replying, "yeah, you get it. It's her life. So, when I bring it up with her and try to explain that none of it makes sense to me, she gets really mad. Well, not mad exactly... more like disappointed. I feel like she listens to everyone else but refuses to hear me." Maera exhaled deeply and looked down.

Moving in a soft circular motion, Evan's thumb continued to stroke the back of her hand. Instead of having the desired effect of soothing her, Maera's eyebrows pulled tighter with concern. "Plus, I feel like she is keeping something from me, and she is refusing to listen to me. It's actually what we were fighting about just before I ran away with the key. She was lecturing me for the millionth time about how I lacked discipline and was rejecting my destiny. I was trying to explain to her how I didn't need to believe in the power of the key to be a better person. I didn't need to unlock some other realm to feel whole."

Maera paused and then snickered at the connection. "But that's exactly what I did when I stole the key, isn't it? I got lost and 'unlocked' the surface. I found the other realm." Maera surprised him with a burst of anger. "And I was right, the surface isn't just some myth. It's obviously real," she exclaimed, raising one hand towards the ceiling of the cavern, lifting her eyes in exaggeration. "And what really gets me..." Evan could feel her rage surging outward like a wave rushing the shore. "What really burns me up is that I get the feeling that she knew the surface was here all along, in actuality, not just as some sort of symbol. And she has deliberately been trying to keep it a secret. It's like she's been hiding the truth behind our people's beliefs. I've always felt that to be so, but never had any proof until now." She exhaled sharply like she was trying to expel her disgust.

Still reeling from her spark of anger, Evan was caught off guard when Maera softened, her rollercoaster of emotions barreling down the track. Her flame extinguished in an instant with a wind of calm tenderness. She reached up to stroke his face. "What's really crazy about it all... aside from my mother's hypocrisy and lies... is that maybe part of it's not a myth after all. You're real, right?" she asked.

Evan felt a few steps behind, and he stumbled to catch up with her train of thought. Did she mean what he thought she did? Was she implying that he might be what she was searching for without even knowing it? The suggestion stunned him. It must have her as well because he thought he saw a flush fill Maera's cheeks. She quickly changed the subject. "My mom is going to be furious at me when I tell her about all this... about you." Her face now filled with worry.

She shook her head, struggling to refocus her thoughts. Straightening her shoulders, she wiped all emotion from her face as if attempting to steel herself for the daunting task set before them. "But before I can return, I have to get the key back. You said you know where it is, right? You can help me get it back, right?"

Following her lead, Evan also stood straighter. "Yeah, my parents said they were going to have one of their friends study it because it's so… remarkable." He couldn't think of a better word to describe it, but that didn't stop Maera from nodding in agreement. "But it's still in our hotel room because they haven't had a chance to take it to his lab yet. It should be easy enough for me to get it and bring it back to you." Evan wasn't sure he believed himself. He tried to visualize the simple mission of retrieving the key. After returning to shore, getting the key back from his parents wouldn't be hard, but persuading them to allow him to go out for another kayak trip would be. His mind paused to plot the next step, and he absent-mindedly bit the skin at the edge of this thumbnail. Maybe if he brought Ross along, he wondered. But this is where the edge of his map went blank.

Afraid Maera would know he didn't have a clear plan, he squared his face with hers and insisted, "I'll figure it out, I promise." Setting down the final details of a plan for later, he attempted to portray confidence by adding, "So, we'll meet back here tomorrow night?" He hadn't meant for it to sound like a question, but the moment he considered it, he began to question the idea himself. He ached at the thought of leaving her. Confused by this new emotion, he was unsure of how it was possible he could feel so attached to her in such a short span of time.

"I want to go with you," she responded, interrupting his thoughts, straightening her body further with courage.

"What, are you crazy? That would never work. How am I supposed to just introduce you to my family? Mom, Dad, Ross…I'd like you to meet my new friend, Maera. She's a mermaid. Her hair glows. That magical key is hers, and she would like it back, so she's coming with us to get it. She…"

"Ok, ok," Maera interrupted again, not allowing him to go on in the ridiculous scenario he was creating. "I get it. So I just have to wait here and trust you'll bring it back?" Her eyes were full of worry as she searched his, looking for reassurance.

Evan disliked her skepticism, but upon considering it from her perspective, he couldn't blame her. She hardly knew him, and the key was obviously incredibly significant. He conceded it was a big leap of faith he was expecting her to make. But wasn't all of this? He still wasn't completely sure that any of this was actually happening. Part of him still wanted to wake up and be lying on the sand next to his family as the sun came up, but the other part of him, the part holding hands with a beautiful girl from under the sea, wanted desperately to impress her. He wanted to be able to make everything ok.

Surprised by a surge of confidence, he suddenly felt hopeful. "I promise I won't let you down. I'll bring back the key." He smiled at her, squeezing her hand to convince her he could.

Maera's eyes searched his for something she could believe in, and a weak smile formed on her mouth. "Ok. I suppose it's my only choice. I'll meet you back here tomorrow night. Can you find your way back?"

Evan nodded confidently, hoping to mask his thoughts that strayed back to the task ahead of him. It was a lot to risk for someone he hardly knew. He would have to lie to his parents in order to get back here before tomorrow night. Suddenly, he remembered they were supposed to drive up to Miami tomorrow, and then fly to Turkey. His parents were scheduled to produce a story on the whirling dervishes in Istanbul. He had been excited about that trip and couldn't believe he had allowed himself to forget. If he came back to meet her tomorrow night, his family would miss their flight. His parents would be incensed and worried too, since he would have to retrieve the key without telling them. He would never be able to tell them truthfully what he planned. "Mom, Dad, I have to help a mermaid get the sacred key back?" He tried replaying the ridiculous explanation with which he had previously mocked Maera. This was going to be a lot harder than he initially thought.

He could tell Maera had heard all of his thoughts, but despite his dilemma, her eyes continued to beg. "Please, I don't know what else to do." Tears collected on her lower lashes. Unable to hold back the worry each drop contained, they spilled in streams down her pale cheeks. Tiny glowing streaks stretched down to the edge of her jaw before dropping to the ground below. Evan could see faintly lit drops mark the sand before they faded into darkness.

"Oh, please, don't cry. I'll figure it out." Squeezing her hand, he added, "We'll figure it out. It will be ok." Evan was surprised by his tenderness and his desire to relieve her pain. Despite the world of trouble, he was going to create for himself, his urge to help her welled up in him like the tears in her. With all the certainty he could muster, he said, "I will meet you here tomorrow night... with the key."

Chapter 8

Evan returned to the beach just as the sky was beginning to lighten and cast a soft pink over the world. It seemed strikingly different from the blue glow of the cavern he had just left. Despite having just left her, his mind continued to return to her. He wondered how Maera's glowing hair would look in the light of the rising sun. Would it grow dimmer in contrast to the brightness of the sun or lose its radiance entirely?

As he emerged from the tangle of mangrove branches, he saw that his family still lay asleep on the sand. The jacket he had left in his spot next to Ross had collected dew during his absence, proof he had not been asleep with them for some time now. Real evidence that the night's events had not been a dream after all. He remained in a state of shock as he tried to comprehend the enormity of what he had just experienced - the undersea world, the merpeople, the mind-reading, the key... Maera.

What was most astonishing was how difficult leaving her had just been. The magnetism that pulsed between them with each look and touch had felt like a force too strong to overcome. Once they had determined to proceed with his plan to retrieve and return with the key, Evan released Maera's hand, but they both stood frozen before each other, unable to move or look away. When she pulled the device from his temple, severing their communication, Evan was jarred by a cold snap that ran down his spine. He felt alone and adrift within his now silent mind. Even though she remained just inches from him, Maera appeared as a mirage, an unattainable hallucination. Could she still hear him?

He nodded once and turned from her. With each step he took towards the cavern's exit, he felt colder and weaker. He was afraid to turn back, fearful that she may not be there if he did, afraid that he would then finally realize it, in fact, had all been a dream. Just before leaving the faint glow of the subterranean room, he looked over his shoulder and saw her there by the phosphorescent pool. Her hands were clasped together before her mouth in silent prayer. He thought he could feel her in his thoughts once again saying, "Please."

As he crawled again on his hands and knees through the low, damp tunnel and towards the surface, he wrestled with his tangled emotions. Confusion, desire, worry, exhaustion, awe - all of these and more had flooded his circuitry, and he was trying to separate reality from dream. She was real. She had to be, simply because of how intensely he felt about her. They hardly knew anything about each other, yet he felt completely connected with her. It was like he was made more complete by her. He smiled at the idea, reminded of the Meram's myth surrounding the key and how it represented the way to becoming your complete self. Maybe there was some truth to it after all.

Ross rolled in Evan's direction, rubbing his eyes open, and he looked up at him. There was a moment when it seemed as if Ross might speak and ask something like, "How long have you been up?" Instead, with the restraint reserved for exemplars like Gandhi, he provided the usual chin-lift of recognition and turned his gaze towards the water as he sat up. Evan sat down next to his brother and shared the silence as the sun rose. Evan was struck by the thought that Maera had never seen this explosion of colors and light that occurred as the earth continued its perpetual turn, marking the beginning of each day. She had never seen a sunset, snowfall, or flowers blooming. As he wondered how the Maeram marked time, he was interrupted by his mother's cheerful "Good morning! Did you boys sleep well?"

Ross nodded in the affirmative before proceeding with his morning stretches. Evan tried to channel some of his brother's discipline and refrain from telling his family everything about what happened last night. He resorted to lying and said, "Yeah, like a baby. I must have been tired out by all the paddling yesterday." Guilt seeped into Evan like cold under a door in winter, but he knew this was only the beginning of the deception which lay ahead today.

"Your dad obviously had no trouble sleeping," his mom teased as she leaned over to kiss her still sleeping husband's forehead.

"Hmmm, what? I'm up, I'm up." His dad responded as he stretched his arms and legs in opposing directions. Rubbing the sleep from his eyes, he said, "I suppose we better get a move on. We're going to have some explaining to do when we return these kayaks a day late. Plus, we'll need to hurry if we're going to make it up to Miami by five this evening." He hopped into action, readying the boats for the return trip.

"You're right," his mom said before inhaling the damp morning air deeply, her eyes closing in an expression of bliss. "But this was nice, wasn't it guys? I'd say it was just what our family needed. A little quiet time to reconnect." His mom came between Evan and Ross, reaching an arm around each son to hug them both at once. It felt nice to have his mother's affection, but Evan knew he didn't deserve it, not now, as he anticipated the deceit he would commit today. "I'm really looking forward to seeing Istanbul with you both. I think you're really going to like it."

"Yeah, me too," Evan said, although he worried he didn't sound genuine enough, so he added, "I'm pumped for the trip." He knew he had overdone it when Ross cast a quizzical look in his direction. "What, I'm just excited," Evan said as he shrugged and turned to climb into his kayak. Ross could always see right through Evan. He didn't need a communication device to read Evan's mind. It had always made Evan wonder if Ross had some sort of telepathic talent, or was Evan merely an open book - easy to read. If he didn't want Ross to detect any more of his lies and ruin what few plans he had so far concocted, he would need to keep his distance. He quickly paddled off in the direction of the shore, trying to figure out how he was going to get the key and get back to Maera.

But then what? After he returned the key, would he just say goodbye and never see her again? A new worry was heaped onto his growing pile of concerns which seemed heavy enough to sink his boat.

Consumed by his swirling thoughts, he was surprised by how quickly he arrived back at the hotel beach. He must have been pulling hard with each stroke because when he turned to look for his family, he could barely make them out in the distance. It wasn't until he stepped onto the hotel's beach that he noticed his fatigue. Two days of vigorous paddling, without a night's sleep, had caught up with him. He felt as though he might collapse. The longer he stood watching his family, who still remained far off from shore, the heavier his body became. Unable to support his own weight any longer, he sat down on the damp seaweed-strewn sand and quickly drifted off to sleep. He awoke with his paddle still in hand. He could smell the stench of rotting seaweed and feel Ross nudging him with his sandaled toes. Ross gave him a deep scrutinizing look as if to convey, "I know something's up with you." Evan tried to force his mind to become blank, but he knew he wouldn't be able to do so now, so he quickly rose to return his paddle to the storage shed without looking back to see if Ross was watching.

While he knew he needed to keep everything completely secret from his brother, he couldn't help but think that if Ross knew about his plan to return the key, perhaps he might be able to provide some help. He could at least provide some cover from his parents. However, he was certain that trying to describe Maera and her undersea world would be impossible. Ross would never believe him and certainly think that he had gone mad.

Then an interesting idea sparked in his mind. Evan wondered if maybe his brother's silence could work to his advantage. Sure, Ross would think he was crazy, but he wouldn't tell anyone. He certainly wouldn't end months of hard work on Evan's mad account only, would he? Likely not, but he probably would make the effort to write it down and tell their parents that he was worried about Evan's mental health. As Evan bounced between the pros and cons of telling his brother, the scales stayed balanced, so he decided it was too big a risk.

Evan's ache to confide in Ross, made him realize how often he had taken Ross for granted. He had missed his brother during this season of silence but knew this wasn't the time to seek his counsel. He did make a note to be a better brother - just not today, though. His deception would have to include Ross.

By the time his parents had arrived on shore, the boys had returned the kayaks to the racks and had finished stowing their life vests in the nearby shed. To accelerate his plans, Evan began dragging his mom's boat up before she had even been able to grab her sunglasses and hat from the bow. "Thanks, Evan. I know we're in a rush, but whoa there tiger! Slow down. You're making me feel nervous," she teased him gently.

"Sorry Mom, I just know we have a lot to do and not a lot of time." Evan swallowed hard on the truth of it. He was still not sure how he was going to swing retrieving the key, sneaking away with a stolen kayak and returning to Maera without his brother or parents realizing.

"It's fine, honey," she assured him, patting him on the back lovingly. "We'll get it all done."

Will I? Evan wondered silently, his heart racing as he thought about the task before him. He wished he could channel some of his mother's optimism, and he was reminded of a yoga meditation class he and his brother had taken in Mumbai. The teacher, an ancient woman with long white hair and deep creases in her tea-colored skin, had instructed them to visualize themselves actually completing the steps necessary to achieve a goal. She had called it the power of positive thinking. But with her accent, it had sounded like *tinking* to him, which always made him giggle when he thought of it. Despite a genuine effort on his part to employ the technique, Evan had never been very good at the practice. He always seemed to be derailed from his train of thought, and he had worried this was a sign that he might never be capable of achieving any goal.

Determined to attain his goal now, he decided to give the positive *tinking* a chance and tried to imagine himself completing the steps necessary to return the key to Maera. He started by imagining himself retrieving the key from the hotel room. He tried to imagine the weight of it now, smooth and heavy in his hands. This had an immediate calming effect, so he continued the practice. He could see himself placing it in the pocket of his swim trunks, feeling the band around his waist pull down slightly on that side from the key's weight. He could picture himself walking coolly out the hotel door, saying "Be right back," and not waiting for approval from his parents. He then visualized casually opening the shed door, taking a paddle and vest. Even though he knew he was a good swimmer and didn't feel he needed it, he wouldn't want to attract any attention to himself and be scolded by some hotel staff or even worse, a passing coast guard boat, for not having a life preserver. He could see himself brazenly lifting a boat from the rack without permission and placing it in the water. He could see himself swiftly paddle away without looking back, hoping no one from the front desk would notice he left without signing out a kayak.

He breathed deeply, smiling slightly with the relief. He thought the yoga instructor would have been proud of him for completing the practice. He was buoyed with confidence at how easy it all seemed, but then felt the crushing guilt sink him down. While the steps he visualized were easy, the lying to his family and ruining their travel plans part was not. He pushed those thoughts from his mind, trying to remain focused on his mission. He could not allow worry to accompany him on his journey today.

"Alright, let's get on with this," his dad said as he clapped his hands once loudly.

Jerked from his meditative thoughts, Evan saw that Ross was still eyeing him with suspicion. Evan lifted his eyebrows, hands, and shoulders toward his brother and mouthed the word "What?" Ross pursed his lips, indicating he knew Evan was up to something, but turned and walked towards the hotel, unwilling to do anything about it now. Evan felt a drop of sweat run the length of his spine. As if in response, a chill ran back up it. He would need to be careful around Ross. He wiped his sweaty palms against his thighs and mimicked his dad by clapping his hands and echoing "Yeah, let's!" He closed the shed door, but not for the last time today.

"I'll go explain everything and settle up with the hotel while you head back to the room with your mom to get cleaned and packed."

His mom squeezed his father's hand and winked one eye. "Good luck," she said with a smile before she walked off in the direction of Ross. Evan nodded to his dad before following behind.

The room was cold because they had inadvertently left the air conditioning running while they were gone. A chill shuddered through Evan as the door closed behind them.

"Brr! Will one of you please turn that off while I jump into the bathroom for a quick shower?"

"Sure mom, no prob," Evan said, but it was Ross that actually was already turning the dial on the box below the window. Evan tried to temper the thrill that now tingled through him. With his mom in the shower and his dad at the reception desk, this was going to be easier than he thought. Even if Ross suspected anything, Evan knew a minor suspicion wouldn't be enough to break his seal of silence. Not yet, anyway, but he would need to get the key first. Before she had a chance to close the bathroom door behind her, Evan asked, "Hey mom, what about the key? We don't have time to get it over to that guy's lab before we leave today, do we? Can I just keep it after all?" Evan looked pleadingly at his mom and tried to conjure a sweet boyish face, hoping to exploit her tenderness.

She sighed, her shoulders hanging heavy. Evan was struck by how old she looked now. Perhaps it was a night spent sleeping exposed on the sand or the amount of sun she had gotten from being in the Keys for the past week that caused this. Her eyes were puffy, making the wrinkles around them appear more pronounced and deeper. Her long, wavy hair had been pulled back in a side braid, but most of the coarser grey hairs had broken loose from all the rain and wind, giving her a witchy appearance. "Oh honey, you're right, but I'm really not in the mood to discuss it right this second. I promise I'll think about it while I'm getting cleaned up."

"Fine, but where did you put it? I just want to look at it again, if that's ok." Evan was relieved that this request didn't seem to attract any interest from Ross, who was methodically folding each article of clothing which he had stored in the hotel dresser and now was placing into his travel backpack. Evan couldn't help but glance over at his pile in the corner of the room. His clothes were spilling from the open pack, erupting like lava from a volcano, hanging down onto the floor in a jumbled mess, dirty mixed with clean. He felt embarrassed by his lack of organization but never enough to make him change.

He looked back at his mom, who said, "Sure. I put it with the passports in the hotel safe. The safe key is hidden under my bag in the bottom of the closet." She closed the bathroom door behind her, and Evan could hear the bath water begin to flow.

Evan walked to the small closet with mirrored sliding doors. Before he even had a chance to look for the safe key, he felt a sinking in his stomach when he saw that the safe's door was slightly ajar. The safe key had been inserted into the slot and remained there now. It was dark inside the closet, but there was enough light to see when he opened the safe fully, that the only things inside were the family's passports. As long as he could remember, his mom had always been the keeper of these valuable documents. She was very careful to lock them up at each of the places they stayed or keep them tucked inside her shirt in a special cloth bag designed for just this purpose. Evan was glad he didn't have to see his own passport very often because he hated the photo. Every time, he looked away nervously when it came time to be inspected by airport security, not wanting to see it but also unsure of how anyone would think the child pictured even resembled the current version of him. He had been thirteen when the picture was taken, so he tried to forgive his awkward appearance, but it was just so bad. His bangs had been cut about two inches too short, causing them to stand almost vertical. His cheeks were still chubby at that time and looked even wider because of his garishly big smile. He had recently asked his parents if he could replace the passport with a new one, but they had sensibly turned him down with the reasoning that he would be able to get his adult passport in just about a year and this one would not expire before then.

"Are you sure it's with the passports, Mom?" Evan called over his shoulder, loud enough so she could hear through the closed door and over the running water.

"Absolutely. I know I put it in there. Why?" she called back.

Evan's mind raced. Why was the safe open? Did someone steal it? If so, how'd they get in the room and into the safe? None of it made any sense. Evan turned to his brother, "Ross, did you open the safe before we left?" Ross shook his head no, cocking his head to the side, furrowing his brow and giving his brother a quizzical look, as if to say, "Why would I do that?"

"I don't know. Are you sure?" Evan was used to talking back to Ross as if he was part of a two-way conversation. Ross just shook his head harder and turned away from Evan to continue packing.

"Mom, would Dad have gone in the safe for any reason?" Evan hollered towards the closed bathroom door.

Peeking her head from behind the door, Evan could see his mom was wrapped in a towel, and this made him blush. "No. You know he never messes with the passports. That's my domain." Evan knew that even when his parents traveled without their sons, his mom still managed his dad's passport. He couldn't think of a time his dad had ever traveled alone, and he wondered what he did with his passport before he met his mom. "Why, honey? Is it not there? I know I put it there and checked the safe before we left yesterday like I always do before we leave the room. It was there then, and I left it locked."

Evan wasn't sure what to do. Should he tell her about the missing key? Would this cause alarm and delay their trip? Or would she just dismiss the lost key as a strange fluke and not let it interfere? It wasn't like she was planning on keeping it anyway, and she always seemed so detached from possessions. Evan felt anger begin to simmer inside. How could she have been so careless as to leave the key to the safe laying under her bag in the same closet? Why did she even bother locking it? He instantly felt guilty over blaming her, but he was frantic about the key. Where was it? How would he ever find it? What would he say to Maera? Panic gripped Evan, causing his breath to quicken. Unable to control his emotions or thoughts, he blurted out, "It's gone, Mom! The safe was open, and the key is now gone!"

"Are the passports there?" she demanded barging out of the bathroom in only her towel. She gently pushed Evan aside to look and sighed audibly with relief when she saw the four documents stacked neatly inside. She turned back at it him asking, "How could it have been opened? And who would take just the key? Are you sure you didn't open it?"

"Yeah, right Mom. I opened it and then in like one second forgot that I did." When he saw the hurt look wash over his mom's face, Evan was instantly ashamed by the sardonic tone he had taken. It was like he had just slapped her with his words. He hated how his anger could hurt his family. He softened by saying, "No, seriously, the safe was open when I looked in the closet. And the key is missing. I swear I didn't take it. Really, I didn't!"

"It's ok, Evan. I believe you. I do. It's just that this is so unsettling," she said as she looked around the room to see if anything else had been taken or disturbed. Ross had perked up and was inspecting the space as well, but his eyes never rested too long on anything, which led Evan to believe it was only the key which had been taken. "Who would have done that? Taken just the key but left our passports? It's just so odd. Do you think housekeeping would have taken it?" His mom crossed her arms and rubbed her upper arms, trying to fight off the room's chill and ease her sense of violation. "Let's get cleaned and packed up, and we'll go check with the front desk. Okay? I'm sure there is some reasonable explanation for this," she said as she placed a gentle hand on Evan's shoulder giving a reassuring smile.

Evan didn't feel reassured. Instead, his mind was reeling, and his insides felt like a storm at sea, churning and crashing. The key going missing was the opposite of reason, and he wondered how she could stand there and calmly say such a ridiculous thing. He felt cold even though he was sweating and noticed his hands were trembling. His mother's voice was slow and soft. "Honey, it's ok. I'm sure we'll figure it out. I certainly don't want to get anyone in trouble, but probably just one of the cleaning ladies took it. Why are you so worried about it anyway?"

He really didn't know why he was so worried. Sure, he had promised Maera to bring the key back. However, if he didn't, and he never saw her again, his life would go on as normal. Wouldn't it?

"You look like you might be sick," she said stroking both his arms now.

He did feel like he was going to be sick. He swallowed hard to fight back sour bile rising in his mouth. He took a slow and deliberate breath and wiped the sweat from his forehead.

He began to panic more, as he realized that his life would never be normal now… now that he had met her. He couldn't just abandon her. He couldn't just move on and forget her. The experience in the cave the night before had forever marked him, and he would never be the same. His breathing became rapid, and his heart raced. What was he going to do? He had to find that key.

"Evan, Evan. Easy." His mom spoke gently. Her hands pressed a bit harder against his arms as she slowly rubbed up and down, a technique she had used since he was little to help calm his roiling emotions. Her face pinched with concern. She spoke even softer, "Evan, love. Come have a seat on the edge of the bed. Take a minute to just breathe."

He allowed her to lead him to the bed where he sat obediently. Man, he was tired! He saw Ross' worried expression out of the corner of his eye and hoped he wouldn't come sit next to him. He needed a moment alone to get his emotions under control and come up with a plan.

"Let me get you a glass of water," his mom said. "You must have just overdone it with all that turbo paddling of yours. You were moving so fast on that return trip, your dad and I couldn't keep up." Handing him the clear plastic hotel cup full of water, she rubbed slow circles around his back. "There. You look better already. Just sit here for a few minutes while I take a quick shower. Ross, dear. Please do us a big favor, and grab Evan a snack from the vending machine. You can grab a five from my pack there by the door."

Ross nodded and was up and out the door as Evan finished his cup of water. A faint taste of chlorine remained, and Evan rubbed his tongue against the roof of this mouth to try and remove the flavor. He took another deep breath and looked up at his mom's concerned face. "I'm ok, Mom. I'm ok. I don't know what hit me. I just felt a wave of sickness wash over me for a second there, but I'm fine now." He could see she was apprehensive to leave him alone, so he added, "Too much sun, I guess. Whew!" He rubbed both hands through his wild curls and was surprised by how damp with sweat his hair had become. He sat up straighter and forced a smile. "Really, I'm fine now. I promise."

"Ok, if you're sure. You gave us a scare there. Just promise me you'll sit here while I take a shower. And if Ross gets back before I'm out, please be sure to eat whatever he brings for you. We both know it will be the healthiest of options available." She smiled a crooked smile and winked at him. Evan smiled in response, knowing it was true and also to convince her that he would be alright. He needed a moment alone to think about what to do next, and he was grateful that it was looking like he would have it. His smile worked, and she turned back to the bathroom. "I'll only be a few minutes. I promise."

Trying to remain calm, he thought through what might happen if he returned to Maera without the key. She would be disappointed and scared, of course. He completely understood her fear of returning home empty-handed. If he had stolen something really valuable from his parents, he knew they would be mad and very disappointed. He would definitely have some serious consequences, but eventually, they would forgive him. He was certain they would never stop loving him. Surely her parents were the same, right?

Sitting on the edge of the hotel bed now reminded him of the trouble he had gotten into just a few months prior. He and Ross had borrowed their parents' rental car without permission. Well, if he was honest with himself, it was really Evan who had taken the keys and suggested they take the car on a little excursion. His parents were documenting an archeological dig in Pompeii and had rented the car for the week. Evan and Ross had been excited about the car because his family usually relied on cabs and public transportation while his parents were traveling for work. This would leave the brothers stranded at the hotel, forced to go about the area on foot. Evan enjoyed the many hikes, both urban and through nature, that he and his brother had taken over the years, but he was excited to see more of the surrounding countryside on this trip. His parents had promised a drive down the coast to Sorrento after they finished their story on some newly uncovered ashen figures. "Frozen in Fire" was to be the name of their feature article. His parents had left just after breakfast to gather the remaining photos and information needed when Evan told Ross of his plan to take the car. He held the keys by the chain and shook them, so they jingled lightly like wind chimes.

"Hey, Ross. Now's our big chance. Let's take the car down to the marina. Mom and Dad won't be back for several hours. We'll have plenty of time." He had thought Ross would instantly shake his head in opposition but was surprised when Ross quickly agreed, cocking his head to one side, lifting his shoulders as he nodded. Evan would have thought he would require a bit more persuasion and be the voice of reason, even if he wasn't using his voice. Evan shrugged and said to his brother in a mocking tone, "Well, would you look at that, you're a teenager, after all."

Evan though he was old enough, didn't have a driver's license in the states, let alone an international one, so he was taking a lot of risks operating the car. He had a general understanding of how to drive. He had the chance to learn on a ranch in Texas, but those had been work trucks on open land without roads. He hadn't been concerned with staying in his lane or avoiding other cars or people. He and Ross had bounced on the overly-springy bench seats, their hands wide on the wheels, smiles on their faces just as wide. The turning on those old pickup trucks had been loose. He remembered having to turn the wheel far in the direction he wished to travel. Driving the trucks had felt more like driving a boat, in contrast to the tight, responsive wheel of the Italian car they were taking out for a spin now.

The cramped Italian streets were filled with bikes, mopeds and pedestrians swarming all around, like ants through a mound. It proved to be much more of a challenge and was very stressful for Evan. Ross, who was rarely ruffled during tense situations, now even gripped the edge of the open window with his right hand and the side of his seat with his left. He sat completely erect as Evan navigated the compact car through the cracked and narrow streets of the town. Evan remembered thinking he sure was glad this car was automatic but then realized he probably wouldn't have taken the car had it been otherwise since he had no clue how to drive a manual transmission. As he pulled into a parking space down by the marina, he released the breath he had been holding for what seemed like the entire drive and heard a high-pitched scraping sound. He and Ross both jumped from the car to examine the damage. They discovered that the side mirror on the passenger side had dragged across the parking meter. The car had a two-inch gash in the metallic blue paint.

"Well, crap!" Evan cursed getting back into the driver's seat and slamming the door as he did. Ross timidly returned to the car, awkwardly avoiding eye contact. Evan fumed the entire drive back to their hotel, angry that they hadn't even stayed to check out the marina before returning to their fate. During the few hours spent waiting on their parent's return, Evan's belly churned with guilt mixed with fury at his mistake.

The two brothers sat perched on the ends of the matching hotel beds, their chins tucked and worried gazes cast downward when their parents finally returned to the room. "What happened?" their dad immediately asked after seeing their postures.

Evan swallowed hard, again wishing that his brother would talk since he had always been so good at making a situation seem not as bad as it really was. "Well?" their mom asked, prodding a response.

"We borrowed the rental car and scratched it," Evan blurted out. "It's not that bad," he added, trying to soften the blow.

Without saying anything, their dad calmly left the room to inspect the damage of the car parked just outside the door. Their mother stood in front of them, arms crossed without saying anything but also without appearing upset. It was as if she was withholding judgment until she had all the facts, which she knew her husband would be able to provide upon his return. "You're right, it's not that bad," their dad said in a tempered voice when he re-entered the room. "But come on, guys! You aren't licensed to drive in Italy. You don't even have your license back in the States! Seriously, what were you thinking? Even if you did have a license, you're not authorized to drive the rental. I mean really, Evan!" His dad paused to close his eyes and take a deep breath before proceeding. "Where did you go?"

Ross remained mute, staring intently at his feet, leaving Evan to do all the explaining. Evan knew he had been the one doing the driving, causing the actual damage, but he would have appreciated a little deflection. "It was my idea. We wanted to check out the marina, and I accidentally hit a parking meter. It's in the dumbest place right at the edge of the curb. I'm sure tons of people have hit it, I mean, how could they not?" At least Ross nodded in agreement at this, providing Evan with a shred of validation. His parents didn't seem convinced that the accident was in any way the fault of the parking meter's poor placement. "I know, I know. We shouldn't have taken it. I shouldn't have," he corrected. "I'm sorry. I'll pay for the damages."

His mom finally spoke. "Thank you, Evan, for being so honest and taking responsibility. We can see you've had time to think about your actions, and you are taking steps at making things right. We appreciate that. Luckily, the car is covered under insurance, so it will be a fairly small fee to fix it, and we do applaud your offer to pay. I think that seems like an appropriate consequence, but you both will split the cost." Evan looked at Ross feeling a pang of guilt, but his brother didn't appear angry at being included in the punishment, even when it hadn't really been his fault. "Now, let's not let this ruin the rest of our trip," she added.

Evan had been relieved by his parents' kind, level-headed response. He realized that most of his punishment had been self-inflicted. He hated disappointing them. They were such good parents who trusted him and wanted what was best for him. He assumed that Maera's parents would be the same way. Surely she would be able to return to them without the key, and they would forgive her.

Framing the situation in this light, he realized that not being able to return the key to Maera wasn't really what was bothering him. What had caused his emotions to spin out of control was the idea of never seeing her again. More than wanting to return the key to her, he wanted to be returned to her. Maybe the key missing wasn't such a big deal, after all, he began to convince himself. The clarity of what he must do now solidified in his mind. His breathing slowed and found its normal pace. He swallowed hard and nodded his head. He would return to her... without the key.

At that same moment, Ross re-entered the room with a granola bar in hand, and his mom peeked her wet head from behind the bathroom door. "How are you feeling now? You look better, that's for sure."

Peeling the wrapper from the bar his brother just handed him, he took a bite and spoke with his mouth full. "You're right, Mom. I am feeling much better. Sorry, I must be really tired from last night or something. Do you mind if I go sit by the water while you and Ross finish getting cleaned up in here? I promise I'll be super quick once you both are finished."

"Of course, as long as you stay in the shade. I don't think you need any more sun." Concern still tightened his mom's brow, but Evan didn't read any trace of suspicion. "Whatever you need to do to feel collected. We don't have much time, but a few deep breaths by the water can be very centering. This has been a stressful few days. It will all work out just fine, though." She smiled at her son and popped her head back into the bathroom, closing the door softly.

Evan couldn't figure out how he had come from such measured, tempered people when his emotions always seemed so raw and rapid. "Thanks, Mom," he said loud enough for her to hear as he walked toward the door. On his way past Ross, Evan noticed a strange look on his brother's face. It was as if he was trying to tell him something. Evan was in no mood to play charades and glibly dismissed him by saying, "This is why people talk, Ross. You might want to give it a try sometime." He let the door slam behind him.

On his way toward the water, Evan passed his father, who was returning to the room. "Hey, I'm going to take just a few more minutes out here to soak it all up before we have to go. Call for me when the shower is free, will ya?"

"Certainly. No problem buddy. I can understand. It sure is beautiful here. Just stay close. I don't want to have to go looking for you."

His parents were always so accommodating and understanding, it hurt Evan to lie to them. "I'll be just down by the shore. I promise Dad." He felt rotten inside. He forced a smile and cheerful wave to mask his deceit. Once his dad was behind the closed hotel door, Evan pushed his guilty feelings deeper down and sprinted to the shore where the boats were kept. He didn't want to waste a second and risk being stopped before he could get far enough away. His parents would be so worried when they were unable to find him. He fought back tears of disappointment in himself at the stress he was about to inflict on them.

Even more upsetting, he thought about how let down Maera would be when he returned without the key. How was he going to explain to her that the key was gone? That he didn't even know where it was? His stomach felt like it had turned to stone, and he had difficulty swallowing. He didn't have much of a plan. He had acted on impulse and bolted from the hotel room at his first opportunity. He now found himself taking a paddle and life vest from the shed.

He tried to settle his mind into the meditative *tinking* practice that had worked so well for him before, but his thoughts were racing. He couldn't visualize the steps to his goal, because he didn't know what they were. All he knew was that he needed to return to her, with or without the key. Of this, he was certain, because it was the only thing that had calmed his panic attack before. He nodded in an attempt to build confidence, and he swung a kayak down from the rack, tossing it into the water in one graceful movement. As he hopped aboard and pushed away from shore, his sureness grew. He would return to her. He felt stronger now. With determination, his speed increased. He flew across the surface of the water. Nothing could keep him from her. The little voice inside him that worried what he would say when he saw Maera was shushed by a fierce conviction to see her again, key or no key. Return to her. Return to her. Return to her. It became his mantra with each stroke.

Chapter 9

Evan's shoulders and upper back burned. His body was spent from his third strenuous paddle across the Gulf. He had only taken one bite of the granola bar that Ross had thoughtfully brought to him, and he cursed himself at not having finished it. It was the only thing he had eaten since the light meal of fish last night, and his stomach scolded him with cramps and moaning. He hadn't thought to bring any snacks along and wished he had grabbed one of the bagels from the free continental breakfast at the hotel. In his quest to return to her, he hadn't wanted to waste any time, and again he had forgotten to grab his sandals; just like two days before when he first found the key and last night when he had chased Maera into the cave.

During the long paddle across, Evan pondered the missing key's whereabouts. He found it hard to believe that housekeeping would have taken only the key and left the passports behind. He had read an article in one of those in-flight magazines about how terrorist organizations had been stealing passports and selling them to bankroll their operations. Not that the housekeeping staff was likely involved with terrorists, but if they were looking for quick money, the passports would be much easier to sell than an artifact so obscure as the key. Also, the maids could have stolen other things of value from the room as well, like his dad's cameras and lenses, but they hadn't. Housekeeping just didn't add up for Evan.

It was as if someone had known the key was in the safe and had gone straight for it. But who other than his family knew about the key? A chill ran through Evan when he remembered the way the old man at the table next to them the night before had lusted after the key. The way his eyes had been transfixed. Thinking back on it now, it reminded Evan of a cartoon character mouse seeing a giant plate of food, and his eyes bulging exaggeratedly from his head as if they were on springs. He recalled how even Ross had been made uncomfortable by the sea captain's stare. Why would that guy be so interested? It didn't make sense. Sure, the key was without a doubt a thing of beauty, but the way the old man had looked so intently, it was as if he knew something about the key that others did not. Did he know its true value? Could it be possible that he knew about the myth surrounding the key? Did he know about the Meram?

Evan knew almost every culture had some sort of mermaid story, but he had never heard of anything like what Maera had briefly described to him last night. He had seen *The Little Mermaid* when he was younger and recalled that Ariel had been his first crush. He had idealized her, with her big blue eyes, long red hair and beautiful voice. He secretly watched the movie over and over, not wanting Ross or his parents to know. He could recite every word from memory, but it certainly was not something that a twelve-year-old boy was very proud of. He smiled now at the innocence of his infatuation. He had a thing for women who could sing. Perhaps because it was what he loved most about his mom, the sweet folk songs she would sing him at night before bed. However, thinking about it like that seemed a bit oedipal and made him squirm.

He had heard other myths about sea-people. When Evan and Ross were young, his mother had read them books about selkies, creatures from Scottish and Irish folklore, who lived in the ocean as a seal but could shed their skin to become human on land. Evan had become lost in imagining what it might be like to inhabit both worlds. After hearing those stories, he would try to hold his breath as long as possible while swimming so that, just for a moment, he might be able to feel what it was actually like to live in an undersea world.

However, in both *The Little Mermaid* and the selkie tales, the merpeople, with their part-human, part-animal composition, were nothing like Maera. Other than her slightly enhanced features, glowing hair, and webbed fingers - he would have to remember to ask her about that - she seemed all human and not fish-like or seal-like at all.

Then there was that book about female divinity in South America his father had assigned Ross and him to read during an extended trip to Peru. Evan had been turned off initially by the subject material and dreaded the paper he would be expected to write, so of course, he procrastinated. Ross, on the other hand, read the book in a few days and promptly submitted a report that his parents had praised for its insight. Evan, who never wanted to be thought of as less capable than his younger brother, reluctantly took the thick book down to the shore. He half-heartedly skimmed the first few chapters, far more interested in watching the villagers mending their fishing nets than reading the dry text.

However, the chapter on Iemanja, the Goddess of the Sea, snared Evan's imagination as if he were caught in her net of seduction. He quickly completed his assigned reading and spent the rest of the afternoon, scanning the internet to find out more about this Brazilian goddess. He devoted his entire paper to Iemanja, typing late into the night. When he gave it to his parents in the morning, his fervor was enough to persuade them to change their travel plans and attend the Festa de Iemanja, which he argued was luckily occurring in only three days in nearby Brazil. During their flight from Lima to Rio de Janeiro, Evan quickly consumed two more books about Iemanja which his mother was somehow able to find in English at an airport bookstore. However, nowhere in any of his reading did he come across any indication that she was part of some larger society of merpeople. Instead, she was described as a deity with supernatural powers of protection, a blend between the Catholic and African religions which was forced to mingle in the boiling pot of slavery.

The night on Copacabana Beach was a peak experience in Evan's life, second only to last night. It filled all of his senses. More than just a New Year's Eve party, the festival brought what seemed like millions dressed in white to the beach to honor Iemanja with offerings. The sand was dotted with altars carved into the sand, filled with burning candles and trinkets. Small wooden boats laden with gifts in her honor were set adrift into the sea to find their way to the goddess deep below. White flowers were dumped into the water in such a volume that it seemed as if the ocean was made entirely of petals. The blossoms undulating on the rhythmic tide danced in beat to the pulsing music which filled the city and spilled out onto the beach. Fireworks erupted casting bright pink, orange, blue and green light across the flowers which carpeted the water's surface. Evan could still remember the taste of the sticky juices from the sweet, stiff fiber he chewed, taking bites from a staff of sugar cane which he bought from a woman's basket there on the beach.

The thought of that sugar cane triggered his mouth to water, and another pang of hunger returned his thoughts to what lay before him. He was unsure how he would summon the energy for yet another voyage back, but he knew he couldn't consider that now, because that would mean leaving her again. The only thing he could think about was returning to her. Return to her.

Return to her. Return to her. He actually chanted it out loud in order to make the last few strokes required to reach the island.

As he dragged his kayak high onto the sandy beach, he turned towards the interior of the island and saw her luminous, pale skin peeking through the tangle of branches.

Chapter 10

He felt his stomach rise to the height of his throat as he stood staring at the vision before him. She looked like a marble statue, carved by some master sculptor and placed here on the island's altar. She stood protected from the burning sun in the shadows of the trees. He could see her eyes squinting to barely slits, unaccustomed to the intense light from the sun. Her features were high and elegant, reminding Evan of classical Greek goddesses he had seen in one of the many museums of Europe. Instead of being hidden by long flowing robes, her figure was accentuated by the outfit she wore. Form-fitting, it was like a second skin, a beautiful slate aqua blue, a color unlike any he could remember. It made him think of the wetsuits he and Ross had worn when they learned to scuba dive, but instead of appearing rubbery, it had a smooth, silky quality, just like the rest of her. He was struck by the beautiful, glowing effigy before him and felt as if he was somehow under her spell. Maybe she was the Goddess Iemanja after all. His frozen state of awe was broken when the weight of dread dropped into his mind. How could he tell her he didn't have the key?

She rushed over to him and gruffly placed a hand on his shoulder, her features sharp and demanding. "What do you mean you don't have the key?" He was saved from the piercing intensity of her eyes when she closed them. She brought her hands to her brow to shield her face from the intensity of the sun. To escape the obviously painful burning rays, she took a few steps back and stumbled over an exposed root and fell to the sand behind her. Evan rushed forward and bent down to her.

"Are you ok? How can you hear my thoughts without the device? And how could I understand you?" He spoke out loud now, as a matter of habit, forgetting she could understand him even without the words. He reached his hands to hers to help her stand and felt a wave of energy pass through him. It wasn't intense like an electrical charge but instead a soothing current of warmth. This sensation only intensified when she placed the gel-like device to his temple. Instantly, he heard her reply.

"Remember, I have the gift." She used one hand to wipe the sand from her legs while holding on to Evan's with her other. "I'm still working on refining my skills, but I can feel people's thoughts from some distance, especially when they are acute like yours were just now. I felt your distress, and I knew right away you didn't have the key." Blinking in a struggle to adjust her eyes to the harsh light of day, she added, "I don't know why you could hear me. Maybe for the same reasons? I really don't know. It's not like I've ever communicated with anyone like you before." Her face screwed up, and her lip quivered as she asked, "What happened? Why don't you have it? What am I going to do?" Tears streamed down her cheeks, leaving faintly glowing streaks.

Even in her current state, dirty and crying, she was still so beautiful to him. He wanted so badly to have the key, to fix everything. He hated letting her down. "I don't know. We will figure something out. I promise."

"How can you promise? Do you even know where it is? Who has it?" Her eyes pleaded, glowing tears still escaping from the corners. Her eyebrows were pulled together, causing her brow to crease. Evan couldn't stop his hand from stroking her face to dry her cheeks. He looked down at his fingers, which glimmered with the streaks of her tears.

Looking back at her, he stood straighter and said, "I have an idea. It may be crazy, but it's all I have to go on." She continued to look intently, searching his face, willing to accept any help he could give. "When I showed the key to my family last night, there was this really strange guy at the table next to us at the restaurant. He was really interested in the key. I mean, the guy wouldn't take his eyes off of it. He gave me the creeps, and I can't say for sure, but I'm guessing he's the one who took it. I can't think of anyone else who even knew about it besides my family. When I left it with them last night, I assume he followed them back to the hotel room and watched through the window as my mom placed it in the hotel safe."

She interrupted him with fear in her voice, her eyes frantically shifting from one of his to the other. "What do you mean, you just left it with them last night, and you haven't seen it since? How do you know they didn't steal it?"

Evan could feel the desperation in her tone but couldn't help but respond on the defensive. "Steal it? Absolutely not!" He felt her recoil at his harshness, and he instantly regretted it. Softening, he said, "I mean, you don't know them. They would never take anything that isn't theirs, and certainly not this key. They knew right away, it was really special and weren't even planning on letting me keep it."

"What? Maybe they have already given it away or sold it. They probably could tell it is worth a fortune." With that accusation, she pulled away, turning her back from him, and he immediately felt a draining sensation. It was like he had been unplugged from her, and he lost his source of power. He felt weak. He reached out and gently touched her shoulder. Instantly, his strength returned.

"No," he was gentle and hoped to be persuading as he explained, "I promise, they are not like that at all. They are good, so much better than me." He hated to admit it, especially to her.

"You've promised before... promised you would bring me back the key, and look how well that turned out!" she snapped back, flipping her head around to glare at him, but now it was her that softened when she saw the hurt look on Evan's face. "I'm sorry. I'm just so scared and don't know what to do. I don't know who to trust. I keep hoping that this is all just a dream, and I'll wake up, and everything will be normal. However, I don't think anything will ever be normal again." She looked down at her feet as she dug her toes in the sand. Evan was reminded of his same thoughts from this morning.

"You can trust me. I know I promised, and I know I have let you down, but I'll fix this. I'll find that guy, and get the key back." Evan burrowed his toes in the damp cool sand to meet hers. Playfully, he allowed the tips of their toes to touch. She smiled as she returned her gaze to his. His hand slid down the length of her smooth arm to her hand. Their fingers wrapped around each other, and he was surprised again by the thin webbing laced between hers, but it did not prevent him from giving a tender, reassuring squeeze.

She allowed her smile to spread more fully and exhaled deeply. "I don't know why, but I do trust you. I only just met you, but I feel so connected to you like I've known you forever. Somehow, I know you will find the key."

Evan nodded, relief washing over him, knowing he felt the same way. He was buoyed by the faith she had in him. The uneasiness, confusion, and fear he had felt since meeting her didn't compare to the peace that being with her provided. Within the span of less than a day, he had met and fallen in love with a mermaid, sworn to retrieve a sacred key, and completely lied to and abandoned his family. When he was with her, he believed he could do anything. He had no idea where the old man was or even if he had the key at all, but Evan felt such an overwhelming ability to find him and retrieve the key.

"You love me?" Evan felt his breath catch when she asked the question.

"Damn it," he thought. When would he remember that she could hear what he was thinking? "I, I, I..." he couldn't finish and couldn't breathe. He felt like he was trapped in a whirlpool, being pulled down by his swirling mind.

She moved her body to close the space between them, and now her lips were so close to his. It was as if she had resuscitated him with her breath, warm and soft against his face. The sweet smell of her enveloped him. He was barely able to accomplish a small gasp of inhalation just before her mouth met his.

He closed his eyes, and everything stopped. The birds stopped their chatter. The waves stopped lapping onto the sand. The mosquitos stopped buzzing around his ears. The earth stopped its rotation around the sun. The electric sensation which Evan had previously experienced merely by touching her was amplified so greatly by her kiss that it sent a shock wave out around them, stopping everything. For that moment, Evan was sealed with a feeling of completeness. It was like she was the key for his lock, and once she placed the kiss and turned the key, something was released from inside of him. A treasure was revealed. She slowly, softly pulled her lips away, but her gaze remained. Birds resumed their song. The tide restarted its ebb and flow. Mosquitoes returned to flight. The earth recommenced its orbit. Evan could breathe again.

He had the sensation he was floating. Often when he was at the beach, Evan would swim out to where he could no longer touch and lie back against the water, allowing the ocean to lull him with her gentle sway, the way a mother might a baby. He would close his eyes and watch the show of fireworks that would erupt behind the darkness of his closed lids. It was as if the screensaver function of his mind had been activated. It would morph between different graphic patterns of light, shifting like a spinning kaleidoscope. Standing here on the solid land, holding hands with Maera, locked in a gaze with one another, he had that same sensation. Eruptions of emotions were blooming within him, shifting from one to the next, as he floated on the flow of energy that was ebbing between them. Overriding all of his feelings was a sense of calm. The temper that usually smoldered deep within him had been blanketed in peace. As the minutes passed, they remained lost in each other, immune to what occurred around them. However, a bolt of fear jarred Maera from their enchantment, causing Evan to turn and see what had arrived behind him.

Chapter 11

"What are you doing here?" Evan yelled at Ross, who was approaching by kayak and making the last few pulls of the paddle to reach the island. "Seriously, Ross! Why are you here?" he demanded in search of an answer, although he knew his brother would never provide the verbal response he wanted. His teeth clenched, and the fire inside him reignited. He felt violated. Maera was his secret, but now, just like the key, she was being taken away from him as well.

Dragging his kayak ashore, Ross gawked with his jaw dropped, eyes wide, shifting his gaze from Maera to Evan and back again, trying to process what he was seeing. "Seriously, Ross, why are you here?" The harshness of Evan's tone was amplified by his aggressive advancement to where Ross stood in ankle deep water.

Evan placed his hand on Ross' shoulder and was about to shove him but, but his impulse was interrupted by Maera's voice in his mind. "You know where the key is? Where? Please, tell me where it is!" However, her questions were not directed toward him this time, but instead to his brother.

Keeping his hand on his brother's shoulder, Evan turned back to Maera and spoke aloud. "What? Are you talking to Ross? You can hear him too?"

Her brow and mouth tightened in concentration, and she craned her head forward as if she was struggling to hear a whisper from across the room. "What man has the key? What are you talking about?" Maera asked her gaze and questions still aimed at Ross.

Like a swinging door, Evan now turned back to look at Ross. "Did I just hear you talk?" Evan asked incredulously. Despite his hope, he knew it wasn't possible, but he was certain he had just heard Ross' voice!

Ross' head shook no, but his reply resonated clearly within Evan's mind. "No, what are you guys talking about?" Ross' face reflected back the puzzled looks of Maera and Evan.

As he struggled to assemble the pieces of their communication puzzle, Evan felt Ross touch his shoulder now as well. Ross had always been one who sought out touch as a way to connect. When they were young boys, Ross would often grasp his older brother's hand before asking a question or crawl in beside his brother in bed and rest his head on his shoulder before falling asleep. Evan never minded and rather enjoyed the closeness he and his brother shared, but he and his brother hadn't been in that habit for several years, not since the day some kid in their grandparents' neighborhood yelled at them as he rode by on a bike, "Are you guys gay or what?" The brothers had been walking hand in hand, which was often their way. Evan had pushed Ross aside so hard in response to the taunt that Ross had fallen and scraped his knee. Embarrassed by what the boy had yelled and more so by responding the way he had, Evan ran away in shame. He hid out in the woods at the end of the street and did not return home until hunger had forced him out later that night. Ross didn't touch him much after that, and Evan missed it. No talking and no touching. His brother had been so far from him until this moment.

"Can you hear me?" Evan heard Ross' question clearly in his mind even though his brother didn't move his lips or make a sound.

The few pieces of understanding he had been able to fit together were now scattered wildly. He must really be tired from a night of no sleep and all the paddling. There's no way he could be hearing his brother. He had just barely begun to accept that Maera's communication device worked. He hadn't considered it might work on anyone else as well.

Evan hadn't heard his brother's voice in months. His desire to connect with Ross had been so profound, so deep, and now, here it was inside his mind. He wanted to hug Ross, tell him how glad he was to have him back. He wanted to jump up and down and celebrate, but his confusion restrained him. The brothers stood with one hand, still resting on the other's shoulder.

"You can hear me? Seriously?" Ross' eyes widened, but his mouth still didn't move. "There's no way... and, what... she can hear me too?" Ross' thoughts streamed.

Like testing the reception of the walkie-talkies they used as kids, Evan responded without words, "You're coming in loud and clear. You can hear me too, right? Without talking. I know, it's crazy, isn't it?"

Ross broke the connection with Evan and placed his face in his hands. Like changing the CB radio to a different channel, Evan lost his ability to hear Ross when he removed his touch. However, he had a pretty good idea of what his brother was thinking still - that none of this made sense.

Maera interrupted impatiently as Ross paced along the shoreline, head still in hands. "Yes, ok, we can hear you without talking. But what about the key? Do you know where it is?"

Ross turned to Maera. Their eyes locked in what had to be a gaze of communication. Evan heard nothing, but judging by the way Ross' eyes tightened with intent around the edges, he could tell he was trying to explain something to her. Evan knew that earnest look from when Ross would try to convince their parents of something. He then heard Maera respond, "Are you sure? Where is he? How do we get the key back?"

"What in the world are you guys talking about?" Evan was the only one speaking out loud at this point. Yelling actually, he was so frustrated. Ross wasn't supposed to be here, on his island, with his secret girl. Ross wasn't supposed to know anything about the key.

He could understand why Maera was quick to accept Ross' telepathic abilities, but he had no idea why Ross was so calm about this crazy scenario. Why did Ross seem so cool about everything? After just discovering his brother on the beach with a glowing girl who could read his mind and he could hers, why wasn't he freaking out more?

Evan clenched his fists feeling like he might boil over. "Come on." He didn't mean for his tone to have as much whine to it as it did. "I can only hear part of the conversation. What are you talking about Ross? Not talking but... you know thinking about? Ugh, you guys know what I mean!" He knew he sounded like a two-year-old throwing a fit, but he couldn't get the words to come out right. He felt even more rage after seeing both Maera, and Ross slightly smile at his tantrum that he actually growled and balled his fist before continuing. "Seriously! I'd like to point out how it would be a heck of a lot easier if you would just talk, Ross." Great, now he was having a conniption fit in front of Maera. What a terrible impression he was making.

The smile on Ross' face fell, and a look of pity took its place. In response, Maera also stopped smiling and suggested, "Try touching him again."

Ross reached up to Evan's shoulder, and the clear connection returned. "Evan, that guy from the restaurant has the key. I know it." Ross' hand remained calm on Evan's shoulder, immune to his brother's fury. "I tried to get your attention before you left the hotel room but…"

He didn't need to finish the thought when he saw Evan's eyebrows raise and his lips draw tightly into a thin line. An "I told you so" expression was clearly painted on Evan's face.

"Yeah, I get it. Life would be easier if I would talk. Never mind that now." With his free hand, Ross made a dismissive swipe through the air and continued his thought. "I followed you all the way back here to somehow explain it to you. I had to. I saw that old man, and I know he took the key. I saw him looking in our hotel window last night before you got back, and again today just as we were returning the paddles to the shed, I saw him walking quickly from the hotel property. He was looking around in this really peculiar way, checking over his shoulder like he was trying to make sure nobody saw him. Then, when we got back to the room, and the key was gone, I knew he had to be the one that took it. I tried to think of a way to make you understand, but before I had the chance you were out the door. I went after you, but man, you were so fast in the kayak, I couldn't catch up. I realized you were headed back to the island, but I couldn't figure out what it had to do with the key." It was only then that Ross began to show some dubiousness about the entire situation. "I still don't get it. Why can you guys hear me? Who is she anyway, and what does she want with the key?" Turning his attention to Maera, he asked, "And why are you glowing?"

"Damn it, Ross. You could have just told me. You know, used words like a normal person. This is important!" He wanted to hit him, push him away, make him leave the island. He probably would have too if his confusion wasn't distracting him from focusing his anger towards his fist. He couldn't make any of it add up. "But you're not wearing the communicator device."

"What communicator device?" Ross looked between Evan and Maera trying to understand. Evan shifted his gaze back to Maera, expecting an explanation, but what he saw on her face was the same puzzled look they all shared.

"I don't know. I can't figure it out either," Maera thought, shaking her head in disbelief. "I would think he would need a communicator device as well. Unless…" she trailed off.

"Seriously you guys! What's a communicator device?" Ross had an uncharacteristic edge of irritation to his tone.

"Unless what?" Evan shouted out loud, although he knew it was completely unnecessary. His harshness caused Maera to recoil. This was the second time today Evan had hurt a woman he cared about with his fury. His shoulders slumped. He took a deep breath, trying to relax. He had always hated his temper and did so even more now that it was capable of hurting her. Trying to take it back, "I'm sorry, I'm sorry. I'm just so mixed up by all of this. Please help me understand. Unless what?" his tone was much softer this time.

"He must also have the gift."

Chapter 12

"So let me make sure I totally understand all this. You live in vast underground caverns that stretch beneath the ocean, use geothermal energy, make your clothes from stretchy fibers harvested from the secretions of the hagfish, and have high-tech breathing devices so that you can go on long swims deep beneath the surface and Evan is using a device on his temple so that we can all communicate with our thoughts? You have legends about 'Landmen' like we do 'Mermaids,' you glow, your mom's the leader, and you stole the sacred key and have to get it back?" Ross took a deep breath to fill his empty lungs after confirming his understanding all in one breath. "Did I miss anything?" He was the only one left standing after what seemed like hours of explaining. Maera and Evan had gone over it all again and again in order to sate Ross' incredulousness. At some point, the exhaustion of the previous night's and day's events had overtaken Evan, and he slumped onto the sand in the shadow of the mangroves. His head was propped on his knees, but his hand careful not to lose hold of Ross' and break their communication. Maera had followed suit several minutes later and sat next to him, her face showing signs of fatigue with darkness below her otherwise bright eyes. The shadows appeared even more pronounced against her fair skin, which was flushed from the heat of midday.

"Yeah, I think that's about it." With a weary tone, she pleaded, "Now please, how do we find the key?" Had Maera known how long Ross' interrogation would take and how deep he would require understanding, she would not have made the deal with him to answer all his questions before he worked out a game plan for retrieving the key.

Likewise, Evan felt that Ross' curiosity had taken them both hostage but knew Ross needed to understand all sides of something before he would relent. He also knew he needed his brother's help if they had any hope of getting the key back. Evan was so tired, he couldn't begin to think of where to start. The good news was that Ross had a mind for strategizing. He could engineer any complex scheme in a matter of minutes, while Evan would still be working out the first step.

"Alright then, let me think," Ross finally released his connection with his brother and began to pace the water's edge.

Evan chuckled as he recalled his brother once saying, "I think better with my feet in water." Ross couldn't have been older than four or five, and they were trying to come up with a way to surprise their parents with an anniversary present. He had abruptly left the planning discussion, went to the bathroom, and filled the tub with several inches of water. Trying to figure out what his brother was up to, Evan had followed Ross upstairs after he heard the water running. As Ross stepped over the edge, Evan asked his brother what he was doing, and that had been his response. Now, Evan's giggle grew into a laugh bordering on hysterical, and both Maera and Ross turned their gazes on him, looking at him like he'd gone mad. "Sorry guys, I'm just so tired. I guess I'm getting loopy." He said it out loud for Ross' benefit, and his brother went back to pacing.

Maera stroked the side of his cheek with the back of her hand. He felt the electricity buzz between them that made him feel lightheaded and flushed. "It's ok, rest," she seemed to whisper softly in his mind. Ross turned away, obviously embarrassed by the display of affection and returned to pacing the shoreline and thinking. "We'll come up with a plan and let you know when we need you. Sleep now," she urged with a tone so soothing it felt like he was being wrapped in a warm blanket.

Evan felt useless, so overcome with the need to sleep that he couldn't resist despite his desire to. He still feared that this might all come to an end when he woke up and realized Maera, and the key were all just a dream. He was terrified of losing her. "Shhh, it's alright. I promise I'll still be here. I'm real. This is real." Evan may never get used to her being inside his mind, but her reassurance eased all his thoughts. He laid back against the sand, just feet from the same spot where he was last night when he had first glimpsed her. Her hand gently stroked his hair. His eyes closed, and his breathing slowed. Floating into his mind with the sway of the tide, was the sweetest, most ethereal tune. A lullaby from another world, her world, lured him off to sleep, like the sirens to the shore. His last thought before drifting off to sleep was that she had such power over him.

He awoke to Ross helping someone into one of the kayaks. Evan tried to shake the sleep from his mind and make sense of what he was seeing as he rubbed both eyes and looked again. Maera looked so different wearing Ross' hat, sunglasses, and a long-sleeved shirt. Not quite the same as an average teenage girl, but more human for sure. Evan jumped to his feet and ran towards Ross and yelled. "What's the big idea, Ross? Where do you think you guys are going?"

Ross reached his hand out to Evan in an attempt to keep at bay his oncoming attack but also took the opportunity to connect and communicate. "It's cool man. It's all cool," his voice was ever calm as if he knew just how Evan needed to be handled. "You've been asleep for a while, and we've worked out a plan to get the key. It will work. I promise. Relax."

Evan looked to Maera for confirmation and heard her reassuring him in his mind. "Ross is right. He came up with a great idea, really. If the key is where he says it is, I think we can get it, and be back to the island tomorrow morning." To be sure he heard her correctly, Evan looked instinctively to the west and saw the sun getting lower in the sky.

"What? Why did you guys let me sleep so long?"

"Well, honestly, this is going to be tricky. It took me a while to work out all the kinks, like making sure mom and dad don't find us in the meantime. For that matter, they may have all the cops in the Keys looking for us right now, since we both just disappeared the way we did. I'm sure they're worried sick. It's not going to be easy getting the key back unseen. I figured if we arrive just as the sun is setting, we'll have an easier shot. Plus, you looked like you could use the sleep."

Evan's stomach clenched at the thought of his parents. He hadn't really considered the fallout from his decision to impulsively return to the island that morning. He knew that it would cause his parents heartache when he'd gone missing and figured they would be furious when he finally did return, but he hadn't gotten further than that. He had no plan for his return trip and dealing with the aftermath. Ross was better at these things, and Evan was glad he'd planned for it. He conceded that perhaps it was for the best that Ross had followed him back to the island, but he still resented having to share Maera with him. The tightening of his stomach reminded him how hungry he was.

"We can get you something to eat when we get back to land." Having Maera read his mind was unsettling enough, but having his brother able to hear his thoughts as well was just too much. The ever-burning smolder inside Evan flared, but his brother's coolness prevailed. "Chill out, Evan. We've got to get going. We're cutting it close as it is. Come on, you're riding with me." Before Evan could protest so that he could be in a kayak with Maera, Ross interrupted his thoughts. "We have to stay in contact if we're going to be able to talk. You still have the communicator device to transmit with her."

Fingering the gel suctioned to his temple, Evan responded caustically, "Well you have thought of everything then, huh? Did you ever consider that just talking might be the most effective way of communicating?" He spat his words at his brother. He didn't wait for his brother's answer as he boarded the kayak. Since it was designed for only one person, he eased his way out to the bow of the boat and perched himself on the spray deck. He figured he would let Ross do all the work paddling since this was Ross' plan after all.

The boat rocked, and Evan quickly had to compensate for Ross as he settled into the main seat. He felt his brother's foot adjoin with the back part of his hip. And as he did, he heard Ross explain, "We're going to tow Maera. She's never paddled one of these things, plus, she needs rest. She didn't sleep last night either, as I'm sure you are aware. Here, you take this." Ross handed him a paddle. "I'm going to need your help to pull if we're going to make it before dark."

Evan gazed back at Maera, who smiled and waved, as the line between the kayaks pulled tautly. "Ross, I think you're right. I'm completely exhausted. I'm going to take just a quick nap. Are you sure you're ok with that?" Maera looked drained and seemed to glow less because of it. Evan couldn't tell if it was just the hat and long-sleeved shirt muting her vibrancy. She closed her eyes and leaned back awkwardly in the kayak before waiting for a response.

"Of course. We've got this. We'll make sure you're safe." Evan added with a goofy smile. He felt selfish, having not considered her needs before now, and softened his defenses a bit as a result. It felt good to settle into a steady paddle. The rhythm of the strokes and the sound of skimming across the water also helped ease his anger.

"You like her, don't you?" Ross ribbed, almost as if in a whisper for just Evan to hear. His adeptness impressed Evan. He was already controlling his thoughts in such a sophisticated way.

Irritated by Ross' question and by his ability to quickly pick up and master any new skill, Evan's peace was short-lived. Like striking a match, his ire was again sparked. He turned away without answering and began to paddle in earnest. The exercise blocked his mind from thinking and from divulging anything to his brother, although, it was obvious he already had. Evan's shoulders and flanks screamed in protest against the return trip. How many miles had he paddled in the past few days? The thought of paddling this distance again overwhelmed him. They would have to figure out a way to get a power boat for when they needed to return Maera to this island.

"I'm working on that plan next," Ross responded.

"Geez, Ross. Can't you mind your own business for a while? I need to be able to have some time to think by myself." Then it dawned on him. "Hey, wait, why can you hear my streaming consciousness, but I can't yours?" He hadn't thought of it until now but realized that Maera could also hear his wandering thoughts, but he could only hear her ideas she intended to convey. The same also seemed true for Ross.

"Yeah, I've been trying to work that out too. I mean, Evan, this is just so much to take in, as you know. We've just discovered a completely different "race" of humans if you will. Mermaids for goodness sake! I'm having trouble wrapping my brain around that. Then, on top of that, she has this device that transmits thoughts so we can communicate without words. It's awesome, obviously, because I'm sure we don't share the same language. However, somehow, I can hear her without the device, while you need it to convey. As if that's not enough to digest, then we add the fact that somehow I can also communicate without the device with her but have to be in contact with you in order to do so. I'm guessing if you took the device off, you and I would break the link because it's not like we've ever been able to do this before." Shaking his head as he exhaled deeply, Ross added, "I can't make heads or tails of any of it. So, you've got me on how it is that I can hear your streaming thoughts, but you can't mine. I keep thinking that at some point soon I'm going to wake up, and man when I do, I'm going to start writing, 'cuz this is going make an awesome story, right?"

"Can you hear her thoughts streaming?" Evan wondered.

"No, but it's weird. Every once in a while, I'll get a flicker of an image that interrupts my mind. I'm assuming it's coming from her, because it's of things I've never seen before - stuff I couldn't even imagine. Some of the images are of people that look like her, but other images are of places that are glowing with this otherworldly light. I get the feeling she's not transmitting them on purpose. I'm not sure why they're coming through."

Evan had seen some of the same images the first time he and Maera had touched in the cavern the night before, but he hadn't seen them since. It wasn't fair that Ross was connecting with Maera. He felt a pang of jealousy, and the muscles in the back of his neck tightened.

"Come on, Evan, you've got to relax. I get that you're into her. I have no plans to get in your way, but please, be realistic. She's a mermaid, or whatever, and you're not. When we get the key back, and this is all over, that's just it… it will be all over. She's going to have to go back to her world, and you are going to have to go back to yours. You need to start preparing yourself for that. I know she's beautiful and all, but there's just no way of making it work."

"Shut up, Ross! You don't know what you're talking about," Evan screamed. Maera jumped in the trailing boat but was already so deep in sleep that she didn't fully awaken. She turned her head to the other side and slumped deeper into the seat. Evan exhaled and softened his tone. "I've had enough of this. I like you better when I can't hear any of your know-it-all comments, so do me a favor, leave me alone until we get back! Ok?" Evan scooched forward far enough so that Ross' foot no longer touched his back. He needed a break from people rooting around inside his mind. He just needed some peace to think. Alone.

He knew Ross was right. He hadn't thought about what would happen after they got the key back. He had pushed that concern from his mind earlier in the day, unable, or more likely unwilling, to consider it at the time. Ross could always get to the quick of the matter. He was a realist. That was why he was so efficient in creating plans. He didn't waste time with his desires but instead made choices based on what had to be done to achieve the desired outcome. Not Evan, though. His emotions consumed him. They were the driving force behind all of his decisions - or rather impulses. Heart over head.

What he desired most was Maera. Perhaps he could persuade her to stay. She was unhappy in her home. She had said so herself. Maybe her world was so bad that she'd want to stay here. Then his mom's voice filled his mind, "Evan, she's not yours to keep." He hated to admit it, but his mom was right. Even if he could persuade her to stay, he was sure his parents would find some way of sending her home or off to be studied. He could hear his parents say, "Evan, she is an incredibly important find. She's part of a culture never before researched - an entire world to be discovered." He knew that would never work.

He would go with her then. He loved his family, but if he was being honest with himself, he had never really fit in anyway. He would be going off to college in just a year, starting his own life. So why not now? It's not like he would be leaving behind any friends. He had none. He had no one really, now that Ross never talked to him. His parents were always busy with work. If he left, he would at least have her.

From the moment he met her, his connection to her had felt so deep, so profound. It was like she was somehow made for him to find. Thinking of the myth she told him, that the surface represented her people's other half, he was reminded of yin and yang. He pictured the black and white halves of the same circle twisting in towards the other with a dot of each other set deep within. Each side represented different characteristics, different worlds. Both halves were unbalanced by themselves. Both were necessary for completing a whole. Perhaps it was true. Maybe he was her other half, and she was his. Her people believed this after all, so wouldn't it be easy enough to convince them of allowing him to stay? Maybe they wouldn't think it was so crazy.

"I was thinking the same thing," she interrupted.

Chapter 13

"What same thing?" Ross extended his leg so that the tip of his toe touched his brother's hip as he looked between Evan and Maera for an answer.

Evan's cheeks flushed with such intensity, it felt as if the skin might tear away. He hadn't realized Maera had awoken. He worried about how much she had heard of his thoughts. As his heart rate quickened with anxiety, she soothed it by responding, "Oh, it's nothing, Ross. Just something between Evan and me."

Anxiety was replaced by pride. Evan beamed at the idea that he was special enough to share something with only Maera, that his relationship with her didn't involve Ross. "Yeah, it's nothing for you to worry about," he added. He instantly felt petty after making such an unnecessary jab at his brother, but he felt relief in knowing it wasn't completely one-sided in his affection for her. He forced the conversation elsewhere. "We're getting close now. What's the plan from here?"

Ross didn't appear to have his feelings hurt by the exclusion and proceeded accordingly. "It should be dark in a few minutes, so let's aim towards that dock down to the right. See it just south of the hotel? There's a canal there that leads to the other side of the island. If I'm not mistaken, the old guy who took the key lives on a boat in a marina off that canal."

"How would you know that, Ross?"

"Well, after you stormed away from dinner two nights ago, the old man didn't let up his creepy interest in the key. It was weird. It was like the treasure he'd been searching for his whole life was there before his very eyes. He even started to freak out Mom and Dad. They exchanged knowing glances, Mom put the key in her back pocket, asked for the check and we promptly left. As we started towards the hotel, I motioned to Mom and Dad that I was going to take a walk before heading back. They were cool with that, of course, but I obviously didn't tell them what I planned, since I'm not talking and all."

"Yeah, yeah, it's not like I'd forgotten, Ross. Get to the point." Evan was impatient with his brother's verbose thoughts. Perhaps because it had been so long since anyone had listened to him, he was feeling overly chatty now. Chatty with his ideas that is.

"Ok, so anyway, I went back to the restaurant and waited for the old guy to come out. I decided to follow him for a while to see if I could figure out what he was up to. Like I told you earlier, I saw him snoop around our hotel room and look into the window. I was hanging back and couldn't see in myself, but I guess that's when he saw mom put the key in the safe or something. Anyway, after that, I followed him to this marina and saw him board this funky old houseboat made out of plywood boards. It's a dump. I have no idea how that shack even floats. I'm guessing that's where he lives, so that's where we're headed now."

"What? You think he stole the key and then just went back to his houseboat to put it on the mantel? Is your plan for us to sneak aboard, and steal it back?" Evan turned his body around to look at Ross and nearly capsized the kayak. He quickly repositioned his weight to keep the boat level.

Ross shifted his weight as well before continuing. "I mean, it's not like he just took the key to the pawn shop today and hocked it and is now on his way to spend his millions. Even if he does know the value of the key, it would take him several days to find a buyer, don't you think? So yeah, that's my plan unless you've got any better ideas."

Evan was frustrated that Ross was always at least three steps ahead. He actually hadn't considered why the old man even wanted the key. Embarrassed, he knew Ross was probably right and admitted sullenly, "Ok, fine."

"What do you think he plans to do with the key?" Maera asked. "Do you think he really knows what it is and what it's worth?"

"I've been trying to figure that out, along with everything else. It's been an information overload kind of day, as I think you can understand, so I'm just working off some theories here. As you briefly described, your people have extensive myths about us Landmen. That's what you call us, right?" Ross didn't wait for Maera's confirmation before continuing. "Well, while I can't attest to being an expert, we have multiple legends about merfolk as well. While clearly, you do not fit the classic description of half-human, half-fish, your people do live aquatic lives beneath the surface of the sea. It's my belief that most myths have some basis in truth if only a small amount. So, perhaps your Landmen stories and our accounts of mermaids aren't so far from reality after all. Throughout the years, our people have probably had sightings of each other and maybe even made contact, like we are now. In an attempt to understand, fill in the missing gaps in information and explain it, we've both concocted elaborate fairy tales and legends. I imagine someone like our sea captain, who looks as though he has spent his life on the ocean, may have a particular interest in such mermaid myths. Perhaps somewhere along the way, he has heard tell of your people's sacred key. Like any legend surrounding treasure, people have wasted their lives in search of finding it. Maybe this guy has been doing just that. I don't know. That's all that I've got for now. What do you guys think?"

Evan again was amazed at how Ross could process all the information he had so far today. From discovering Maera to communicating without speaking and searching for a lost sacred key, he could keep track of it all and still clearly see the motive for the sea captain stealing the key. Evan felt a warmth of pride well up in his chest at his brother's intelligence.

"Yeah, but what do you think he plans to do with the key?" Maera was obviously keeping up with everything as well.

"Of that, I'm not sure. It's not like finding a treasure chest full of gold, I imagine. He'd have to find someone else who knew it's worth and who was willing to pay him for it if he planned to profit. However, perhaps he's the kind of guy for whom there is enough glory in just finding the treasure." Ross began to back-paddle on the port side, slowing the kayak and turning them towards the entrance of the canal on the left. "I guess we'll find out soon enough."

Chapter 14

Darkness fully blanketed the canal just as they arrived in the marina. However, the night would not be enough to fully cloak their approach with the glow emanating from under the hat which Ross had loaned Maera. Perhaps the nap had helped revive her, or maybe it was just in contrast with the surrounding darkness, but the light radiating off Maera was amplified as it reflected off the water around them, making her appear to be a beacon that was being pulled behind their kayak.

Ross' eyes widened, viewing Maera for the first time at night. Her radiance was breathtaking. "Oh my," Evan heard his brother contemplate breathlessly. A swell of possessiveness rose within Evan. As it rippled out towards his brother, Ross shook his head as if trying to loosen the hold Maera's beauty had taken on his mind. The motion apparently worked, because his shock didn't delay him any longer and he quickly turned the kayak and paddled under the dock. Ross' thoughts hushed to a whisper, conveying they were operating in stealth mode. "We'll tie the boats up under here, and sneak along dockside... without you, Maera. You'll have to wait here."

"No. I'm coming with you," she insisted.

"Well, if you have a way to turn off your glow, then maybe. However, as it is now, I'm certain we would be noticed." Ross lifted his eyebrows as he waited to see if she had a way to control her radiance.

Maera gazed down at her glowing pale hands and sighed, then sheepishly admitted, "No, I can't. The glow comes from our diet. I imagine it would take weeks to wear off. I don't know. I've never tried and don't know anyone who has either." Her shoulders dropped in disappointment. "You're right. I'd blow your cover and draw too much attention. Just be quick, please. I don't like the idea of being out here alone."

Evan didn't like the idea of leaving her either, but not enough to let Ross go by himself, and be the hero who recovered the key.

"We'll hurry. I promise. We'll find the key and come right back. This will all be done soon." Evan wasn't sure who he was trying to convince more - Maera or himself. He had to swallow hard for what felt like the hundredth time today to keep the bile in his stomach from coming up. His ever-increasing hunger, combined with his vacillating emotions and growing nervousness was becoming too much for his body to handle.

"Maybe he'll have some food inside the boat that we can grab along with the key," Ross suggested as he reassuringly squeezed Evan's shoulder. This thoughtful reminder that Ross was there for him strengthened Evan. Ross nodded at the positive effect he had on his brother and proceeded. "Come on. We can do this." The boat wobbled as Ross moved to a squat and reached around the edge of the dock. Without a sound, he pulled himself up and on top, out of view.

Evan looked at Maera, frozen in the beauty of her icy eyes. The light broadcasting the distance between them felt warm as it reached his skin despite its cool blue glow. As he breathed deeply, preparing to join his brother, Maera reached for the line connecting their kayaks and pulled his to her. Hand over hand, she pulled the wet rope, closing the distance between them. Her gaze did not break from his. "I can do this. I'll get you the key. I promise," Evan said as he reached her.

Her fingers touched the side of his neck as her thumb brushed the edge of his lips. "I know you will. I trust you." The electrical current returned, buzzing throughout him between them - as if she was connecting his circuit. She leaned closer pulling him toward her. Just as their lips touched, he leaned too far, and his kayak slipped out from beneath him. The night water was a cold shock. He scrambled, splashing in the water. Maera's hand covered her mouth, but she couldn't hide her laugh.

Ross' one hand reached down and grabbed the back of Evan's shirt as the other extended out for him to take. Using both, he pulled Evan up onto the dock. "What the heck was that all about? Did you miss the part of the plan where we are trying to arrive unnoticed?" His scolding tone softened as he added, "Are you alright?"

Soaked and completely embarrassed, Evan couldn't suppress his smile as he got up, thinking of the kiss with Maera. "It's cool. I've got this. I'm getting her that key back." He felt more confident than ever as he began to stride down the dock.

Ross jogged to catch up and again grabbed the back of his brother's shirt. "Well, that's cool. I appreciate your confidence and all, but don't you think we should at least head in the direction of the sea captain's houseboat? It's that way," Ross added, pointing behind him.

"Fine, you lead the way. I'm just ready. That's all."

"You're something, alright," Ross jabbed as he turned and headed down the dock in the opposite direction.

As Evan followed behind, he felt Maera wish him, "Good luck. Come back soon."

The causal, inconspicuous walk Ross had used until now shifted as he hunched to conceal himself behind the side of a boat. Evan followed suit and crouched beside him. Hiding there quietly, Evan could hear the sound of each drop that fell from his soaked shirt as it struck the wooden dock. He contemplated removing his shirt, but Ross squeezed his hand and shook his head. "It's not that loud, really." Evan nodded acceptance. He appreciated having his brother back in communication with him, but he would never get used to the feeling of Ross inside his mind.

As they peered over the deck of the sailboat they were kneeling behind, his pulse quickened upon seeing what had to be the sea captain's houseboat. It was even more ramshackle than Ross had described. True, it was constructed of sheets of plywood, but it looked more like a kid's clubhouse floating on water than an actual boat. Evan half-expected to see a "No Girls Allowed" sign nailed to the door. The layers of the boards were peeling back, like the lid of a sardine can, warped by years of sea, rain, and sun. To prevent the floating box from coming apart at the seams, supporting planks of various widths and lengths were buttressing the plywood panels. These were held in place with long nails that were half-way hammered in, bent and folded down. Evan wondered how many of them actually made it all the way through the boards. So many of the nails were mangled and slammed into such awkward, frustrated angles. The structure had one small window that had a board running diagonally from the upper corner to lower. Evan couldn't imagine why. This guy was obviously no carpenter.

Evan felt Ross's hand cup into his like it had so many times before as boys. It felt reassuring and safe. However, for Ross, it was more likely for the sake of practical communication rather than comfort. Evan heard his brother's thoughts, "There's no light on inside. That's a good thing. Hopefully, the old guy isn't home."

Evan was encouraged by the support his brother's touch gave him and felt brave enough to suggest they act now. "So let's get in there and get the key then."

"I wonder if we should circle the marina one more time first. Just to make sure there's no sign of him." Ross sounded unsure.

Evan knew he was always more impulsive than his brother and was tempted to agree with the more cautious plan. However, time seemed to be of the essence. "We could, but wouldn't we be risking running into him or worse, running into the cops, who I'm sure Mom and Dad have out looking for us right now? I think we get in and get out. Maera is waiting on us."

"You're right, I suppose. I hadn't considered the cops," Ross conceded. Evan wondered if it was the first time he had ever thought of something before Ross did. He made a mental tally - Evan: *one*, Ross: *one million*. He smiled at his own joke and thought he saw Ross smiling too. "What if he's inside though? Maybe he's asleep," Ross said recentering the conversation on the task at hand. He sounded nervous.

Fearful that he would succumb to his own rattled nerves, Evan felt he had to be brave enough for the both of them. Whether he believed himself or not, he reasoned, "Well, chances are he didn't go to bed early. I mean, it's probably only just after eight, but I doubt he's in there just sitting in the dark. Let's assume he's not in there, and make our move as quickly as possible."

"Alright. Sounds reasonable enough. Let's go." Ross didn't release his grip on Evan's hand as they crept around the stern of the boat behind which they had been hiding. Their hands tightened as they approached the back deck of the dilapidated houseboat. It resembled the back porch of a cabin with a sagging screen door. The screen around the other two sides was torn and poorly repaired with what looked like twist-ties from garbage bags. Evan wondered what good such a screen would do against the mosquitoes that were so thick at times. As they got closer, a smell assaulted them, causing both of them to cover their noses and mouths with their unoccupied hand. It was rank. Simultaneously bitter and sour, it caused Evan's eyes to burn. This time he couldn't control the bile rising. Saliva flooded his mouth, and he retched over the side of the dock. Disturbed by the contents of his stomach, which wasn't much after not eating all day, comb jellies flashed in a cloud of polluted water. Wiping his mouth with the backside of his hand, Evan asked, "What in the world is that smell?"

"I have no idea, but holy cow, it's horrible! I feel like I might be sick too." Ross' hand was still covering his nose and mouth, and his eyes were pinched in disgust. "Where's it coming from?" he wondered as he searched the boat for the cause of the offending smell.

There was nothing visible on the back porch of the boat that would obviously be causing the foul stench, and it seemed too strong to be coming from inside. The roof, Evan wondered, as his chin lifted, and he raised to the tips of his toes. Unable to see on top, he scanned the boat and noticed a makeshift ladder sloppily screwed to the side of the structure next to the screen door. He broke free from Ross' grasp and proceeded up the planks, which wobbled under his weight. He worried that the top board would pull free from the one screw holding it to the wall, but he managed to hoist his body high enough to see onto the roof of the shack. "Well, I'd say I found the source of the smell," Evan whispered, so his brother could hear them now that they weren't touching.

Ross reached for Evan's foot to prevent him from speaking again, nervous that even talking in a whisper would be too loud. Evan was thankful for the timing too because just at that moment, the bottom plank of the ladder came free. Evan's hands gripped the top edge of the roof as Ross swiftly grabbed his legs, supporting him just enough that he didn't slip and fall. Ross quietly lowered Evan down to the dock, questioning as he did. "What's up there?"

Not quite sure how to explain what he'd seen and certainly not sure why it was there, Evan again felt like he would be sick. He swallowed hard again, "It's a rotting alligator corpse."

"What? Why?" Ross looked at him with a puzzled expression.

"Why would I know that? This guy is obviously bonkers, that's why?" Annoyed by Ross' questions, despite having thought the exact same ones, Evan just wanted to get this over with. "Come on. We're wasting time. Let's get in there, get the key, and get out of here. This place and this guy freaks me out." Evan couldn't allow himself to ponder what kind of person lays a dead alligator out to rot on top of his boathouse. If he had, he would have thought twice before grabbing the handle to the screen door and pulling it open, causing the hinge to creak loudly. The sound seemed to echo throughout the marina.

"Shhhh!" Ross scolded, actually making the sound as the airbrushed across his teeth and lips. Evan might have been more shocked by the first utterance his brother had made in weeks, but he was too edgy about their current situation.

Instead, he snipped back, "Oh, yeah, sure, next time I'll be sure to grease the hinges before sneaking onto the porch of a deranged sea captain's dilapidated houseboat. Good point, Ross. I'll be quieter." Evan hated how he was so quick to default to bitter sarcasm, especially since he could tell it hurt

Ross' feelings. "I'm sorry, I'm just nervous," he tried to soften his tone. "You wait here, and keep a lookout while I go in and find the key, ok?"

Ross nodded. "Be careful. We don't know what's in there or what this guy is capable of." He squeezed Evan's shoulder before he went in.

Just inside the porch, there were three steps down which moaned against his weight as he lowered himself down to inspect the door. A hatch constructed from two large boards blocked the entrance to the houseboat. At the seam of the two boards was a padlock which was threaded through two brass loops on either board. Evan's shoulders sank in disappointment. He wondered why he had thought he might be able to just walk right in and take the key. How naive could he be? Of course, this guy would lock his door. He felt stupid, and his rage rose from within. Impulsively, he kicked the hatch out of anger, and as he did, one of the brass loops pulled slightly free from the rotting wood. He grasped the loosened loop and wiggled it, loosening it a bit more. With one swift pull, the brass loop dislodged completely and hung from the padlock which was now only connected on the other side. Without much effort, Evan wiggled the board from the opening and set it to the side. He felt a rush of confidence. "You can do this," he whispered to himself.

While not as horrible as the smell of the rotting alligator on the roof, the odor inside the houseboat was still offensive. Stale cigarettes and mildew mingled within. He placed the back of his hand under his nose to block the smell. Luckily, the space was small, limited to only one room about ten feet square. If the key was in there, he would find it in no time.

He stepped inside and scanned the area. A bare, twin-size mattress lay on the floor in one corner with a sheet and blanket piled on top. He figured the key was likely not there, so he shifted his attention to the opposite wall. A small bank of cabinets hung on the wall, two without doors. A meager collection of dishes and cups were stacked inside one of the open shelves, and the remainder sat unwashed in the tiny plastic sink. Beside that was the countertop, only big enough to allow for a cutting board which still had the remains of a fish. It looked as if it had been grilled and recently picked cleaned based on the fact that it didn't smell horrible. Evan thought the key might perhaps be in one of the two drawers that were contained in the lower half of the cabinets, and he would have started his search there if the desk just to the left of the hatch hadn't caught his eye first. As his gaze fell across the mess of papers and various lures strewn about the desk, that's when he saw it. There was the key! A buzz of excitement shot through him. Maera's key was sitting unhidden on the center of the desk.

His fingers stroked the large pearl on the top end just as he heard Ross' voice call his name in a loud whisper. "Evan! Get out here. Now!"

Chapter 15

Evan grabbed the key and shoved it into the pocket of his swim trunks before crawling back up the three steps on his hands and knees. He remained crouched on the porch of the houseboat as he whispered back, "Ross, did you just talk? Out loud?"

Ross had been holding open the screen door the entire time Evan had been inside so that it would not make the horrible creak again until it was time for them to make their exit. He reached onto the porch and pulled Evan's hand towards him. Without talking now, Evan heard him insist, "Not now. We've got to get out of here. Now! I heard footsteps heading this way."

"Ok. Let's swim back to Maera then, so we don't run into whoever it is that's walking towards us. I'm already wet, and it's the safest way. Follow me." Evan shoved the key deeper into his pocket and quickly lowered himself through the space between the boat and dock, down into the inky water, trying not to splash.

Ross' hand touched his before he released the dock. His eyes looked worried as he asked, "Did you get the key?"

Evan beamed, "Yeah. I did. So let's get out of here."

Ross dropped into the water beside Evan just as the screen door slammed. Both boys ducked under and swam as far as they could in the direction of Maera, remaining below the surface, holding their breath for what seemed like several minutes. Evan was first to come up for air and was impressed at how far they had come. Ross' head popped up just behind his, and the two silently slipped under the cover of the nearby dock. They continued the rest of the distance concealed beneath the path of wooden planks above.

The water smelled of fuel and rotting fish. Evan considered how dangerous it was to be swimming in the marina at this time of night. He wondered if sharks came into the harbor in the evening to feast on the smaller fish who sheltered under the boats and by the pilings. He forced the worry from his mind and pushed forward. All that mattered now was getting back to Maera. Return to her. Return to her. Return to her. It became his chant again, repeating it with each kick of his legs.

Careful to remain hidden under the docks, the brothers swam the maze-like route back to where the kayaks were docked. Evan's shoulders burned with each stroke as he pulled back against the water, but he didn't let his fatigue slow him. He felt as if he was approaching the finish line at the end of a long race. It had been a marathon of a day - the longest of his life, in fact. Since glimpsing the flicker of Maera's light within the tangle of mangroves the night before, he had been barreling through a course, pushing himself to his limits, both physically and emotionally. Here he was, at the end, and he was about to win the race. He had found the key for her. His muscles screamed in protest now, but that only made him kick faster and pull harder. He refused to acknowledge his pain and exhaustion. He focused his mind on only one thing - Maera. He pictured her soft blue glow when he closed his eyes. It filled his thoughts, and with each stroke, he imagined her light growing brighter, more intense.

As he rounded the last turn, he lifted his head above the surface, expecting to see her light reflecting off the black water beneath the dock, but the kayaks sat motionless in the dark corner of the boatyard. She wasn't there.

Panic flooded Evan. He stopped swimming and looked around frantically. He reached his hands to the rough boards of the dock above and heaved his body up from the water. He popped his head from over the edge of the decking but struggled to pull the remainder of his fatigued body any further. He felt like he weighed a thousand pounds. Looking from side to side, there was no trace of her, no faint glow in any direction. There was no movement anywhere. He dropped back into the water to look again under the dock. Maybe he had been mistaken. Maybe he was in the wrong place. Maybe she had been frightened and had decided to hide, but no, the two kayaks were right there, secured where they had left them. She wasn't there. He called out to her in a hushed scream. "Maera! Maera! Where are you?" He spun in circles waiting for a response. He saw Ross in the distance, swimming at a slow and measured pace, closing the space between them, but there was no Maera.

She was gone. The additional weight of it seemed impossible to hold. Where could she be? Did someone take her? How would he find her? Overwhelmed and unsure what to do next, he struggled to stay afloat. It felt as if he had bags of sand tied to his ankles. His arms and hands feebly grasped at the water around him. He pulled and kicked, but he felt himself slip deeper into the water. He arched his back and tilted his head so that his mouth and nose could continue to collect air, but water found its way in despite his efforts. He coughed and spit, but the weight of his tired body continued to pull him down deeper and deeper.

He felt the fight leave him, and he let go. He sank below, allowing the water to wrap him in a wet embrace. It pulled him lower, and he plunged faster as all the air left him. His feet settled against the spongy bottom. The muck reached up and seemed to suck him even deeper. He was letting the depths take him now. Maera's light was gone, replaced by the blackness pulling him down.

Just as he felt he might surrender to sleep in the warm, wet, dark murkiness, he felt a hand fumble against his face. It grabbed him by the hair and pulled him upward, hard. Stronger than the grasp of the dark water, the hand yanked him to the surface. He was like a rag doll as Ross flung him up and over the edge of one of the kayaks. Muffled like a voice screaming underwater, he heard Ross' voice scream into his mind with panic. "What's wrong with you? Did you hit your head or something? Are you ok?" Ross' hands firmly gripped his shoulders and shook him hard. He slammed his brother against the boat. Evan's chest smacked the hull, and life was forced back into him, awakening him from the dark trance that had almost taken him. Ross' voice inside his mind was louder now, and he heard his demand clearly. "Evan, answer me, damn it! Are you ok?"

Revived, Evan clung to the kayak and gulped at the air. He again frantically looked around for Maera. Maybe he had been wrong, and she had actually been hiding, but she still wasn't there. Hot tears poured from his eyes. Unable to catch his breath, Evan alternated between sobs and gasps. His panic grew, and his sobs swelled into a wail. "She's not here! She's not here! Ross, what do we do now? Where is she?"

"Shhh," Ross soothed, rubbing Evan's shoulder. Again out loud, Evan noted, but it was obviously still not the time to discuss how Ross had been slipping in his resolve to remain silent. Having noticed himself, Ross corrected and communicated through his touch, "I know she's not here. It's ok. I'm sure she's close by. We'll find her." His tone was reassuring and had the desired effect on Evan, who could now feel the air enter his lungs, extinguishing the fire that burned there. His breathing grew deeper.

The tears still flowed, but Evan felt his heart rate slow as his hysteria notched down. "But she's not here, Ross. I have the key, but she's not here."

"Evan," his tone still calm and soothing, "We have established she's not here. We now need to develop a plan to find her. The sooner you focus, the more quickly we can do so and therefore, the sooner we will find her." Ross' hand still stroked Evan's shoulder in the way their mother did when she consoled him during his many fits.

Despite feeling jealous of his brother's ability to adeptly manage his emotions and quickly center on a solution, Evan allowed himself to be assured by Ross. He knew Ross was right. He was able to compose himself with one final deep breath. He wiped the tears from his eyes, but his face remained wet as their bodies still floated beneath the docks. "Ok, you're right. We need a plan, but the first step has to be to get out of this water," he said as he pulled himself up onto the kayak.

Ross climbed onto the other boat but placed his hand on top of Evan's to remain connected for communication. He giggled, "Yeah, the last thing we need now is to get eaten by a shark or something. I felt like bait swimming through the dark water just now."

Evan snapped with a spike of rage, "Ross, come on. I'm in no mood to laugh. This is serious. Maera is missing!" He was finding it impossible to keep his emotions in check, and he struggled to respond, "I'm sorry. I'm just so freaked out, and I'm just so tired." He took several more calming breaths. "She wouldn't just wander off. I know she wouldn't. I have this horrible feeling that someone has taken her." He had to swallow back the tears which were welling up again. "How are we going to find her?" Defeat seemed to weigh on him like a boulder. "I don't think I can do this." His exhaustion was overtaking him, and he felt unable to wrangle his feelings, which were wildly bucking within him.

Ross could feel Evan's struggle and squeezed his hand firmly. "I know you're tired and scared. I totally get it. But I know we can find her. We've gotten this far. You have the key, and you're almost to the finish line."

"But I thought this was the finish line... getting back to the kayaks, bringing Maera the key. I thought I'd made it." Evan wanted to believe Ross' optimism but felt petulant at how unfair it all was. He didn't feel strong enough to carry on. "We don't even know where she is now. I don't even know what to do next." Evan looked pleadingly at Ross. He needed him to have a plan.

"I only have one idea, but at least it's a start." Ross paused as if he was unsure if he should continue, his eyes full of worry, afraid that he might set off his brother again.

"What? Come on. Tell me what we do now." Evan urged.

"If you really think someone has taken her, I think the place we start looking is back at that old guy's houseboat."

"What? You mean back at that shack? No way! You said you heard someone coming anyway. What if he's there now?"

"Exactly. I think that one possibility is that the crazy sea captain, on his way back to his boat, saw Maera glowing under the dock. He may have grabbed her and taken her back to his boat. Perhaps he wanted to hide her along with his other treasure." Ross could see the panic surging up in Evan, whose mind instantly flashed to the rotting alligator corpse on the boat's roof. He squeezed Evan's hand more tightly, preempting another attack of emotions. "I'm not saying for sure that's what happened. Obviously, I don't know, but I am saying that I have no other ideas and that is just as good a possibility as any we have now. Do you have any other theories?" he queried but didn't wait long enough for Evan to respond before continuing. "I am certainly willing to entertain other possibilities, but I do think we need to act quickly because if he does have Maera..."

Evan didn't want to think about how Ross might finish that sentence, so he interjected, "Ok, ok. Let's get over there. Are we going by boat or dock?"

"Well, I think we'll be quieter by boat, don't you think? No footsteps to be heard approaching, and both are just as quick. Plus we'll then be able to make a quick getaway." Evan didn't wait to hear more, broke the connection, and began paddling, but Ross grabbed his arm before he could get very far. "However, we can't communicate if we go by kayak."

Evan's temper flared, "Damn it, Ross! Make up your mind! Fine, we'll walk, but have you considered that maybe now would be a good time to give up your dumb silent act. This is bigger than just you!" He slammed down the paddle, jerked himself up onto the dock above and started off in the direction of the houseboat without waiting for Ross. He broke into a run, but when he heard Ross trotting behind him, he slowed, turned and motioned to Ross to be more quiet, knowing he should do the same.

Ross caught up with him and took Evan's hand. "I know, you're right. This is way bigger than me. I'm sorry."

"Not sorry enough to talk," Evan grumbled back, but he knew it wasn't the time to be angry with Ross. He needed him. He also needed to save what little energy he had remaining, and stay focused on finding Maera rather than stoking his own blaze of rage. Lastly, he conceded that communicating without words would be helpful in remaining stealthy. "So what's the plan if he does have her?"

"I don't know. I was hoping you would know what to do," Ross admitted.

"Well… I mean… Hell! We take her back, that's what." Evan was impressed by his own boldness but unsure of how to back it up. He felt certain he would do whatever it took to save Maera but struggled to shake the fear that pricked up the back of his neck. Thinking back to the rotting alligator on the roof of the shack, he wasn't so sure who they were about to go up against.

Chapter 16

The smell met them before they rounded the corner of the dock, which led to the old man's houseboat. A night wind was picking up, dispersing the stench. Ross covered his nose with his free hand and cleared his throat. "Dang, that's awful."

Evan could actually taste the smell as it clung to the particles of moisture in the humid night air. It reminded him of maca, the potent fermented fish smell that permeated the streets of Ho Chi Minh City. However, this stench was far more putrid. "I still can't figure out why he would have a dead alligator up there. Who does something like that?" Answering his own question, he continued. "Only a crazy person, that's who. This guy freaks me out." He squeezed Ross' hand more tightly and straightened his back in preparation for the encounter. "I'm hoping he doesn't have Maera but at the same time hoping he does, just so we can get her back." Evan squeezed his eyes shut. He stopped, put his hand to his head, and tried to steady himself. He struggled to fight off a wave of dizziness. "Ugh, I feel... not right." He shook his head to try and clear his swirling mind.

"Do you need to sit down? We can take a second." Ross put his arm around Evan's back for support. "If you think about it, you've been awake the better part of twenty-four hours, with only one cup of water and one bite of granola bar today."

"You don't need to remind me. My stomach and my head have been screaming at me all day." Evan rubbed his forehead. "No, I have got to do this. I can't stop now. I'm afraid I might not start back up if I do." They continued on. As they closed in on the boat, Evan could see through the single window that there was a light on inside which wasn't before. "Well, at least we know he's in there now. Come on, let's sneak up to the window, and see if we can get a look inside."

The brothers crouched and proceeded slowly, carefully shifting their weight along the boards of the dock. However, it was impossible to advance without the weathered wood groaning and creaking. Evan hoped the noises wouldn't be noticeable above the other ambient sounds of the marina - sailing lines clinking against the masts, the water lapping against boat hulls, voices and laughs from several docks away where people were hanging out and enjoying drinks.

Evan squatted below the window and peered inside as Ross joined him. "Oh man, Ross, she's in there! He has a bag over her head!" The panic was building in him again, and his breath quickened. He saw her straighten up and crane her neck around as if trying to see through the fabric cloaking her head. "Ross! He's got her hands tied behind her back!"

"Evan! Ross! Is that you?" He could hear her frantic tone transmitting through the orb that remained affixed at the side of his head.

Before he had a chance to answer, Evan could hear Ross assuring her. "Yes, Maera. It's us. We'll find a way to get you out. Just hold on!" His tone was level and smooth, like the one you would use to soothe a wounded animal. Evan could see Maera nod her head and adjust her legs beneath her with anticipation. He could feel her pulse racing in pace with his own.

Evan jumped to a standing position, ready to take action. He had to get in there and save her, but Ross pulled him back down with a hard jerk. "Hold on! Take a second to think. He's not in there. So that means..."

Evan couldn't see the point in delaying any longer and didn't let Ross continue. "I know. We have to act fast. Let's get her and go!" but before he could stand again, he heard the click of a cocking gun.

"Not so fast, hot shot." His voice was deep and coarse. "Do exactly what I tell you, and no one gets hurt. Do you boys understand me?"

Ross squeezed Evan's hand so hard his nails bit into his skin. He didn't have to say, or rather think, anything for Evan to know Ross was as terrified as he was. "It's going to be ok. We'll be alright." Evan was the one trying to soothe Ros now, but he doubted his attempt had the same effect. He could see Maera stiffen like water frozen in winter in response to the brothers' fear. He knew she could hear them, even at this distance, so he was desperate to keep his alarm in check.

"Evan, he has a gun!" Ross' thoughts quivered with fear.

"I know, I know. I'll figure something out. We'll be ok." He was trying to convince himself as much as Ross. He kept his eyes set on Maera, kneeling on the filthy mattress with her hands secured to the leg of the heavy desk, a dark pillowcase over her head. He worried that if he took his eyes off her, she might disappear again.

"Did you hear me?" His voice was deeper and harder as he talked through clenched teeth. "I asked if you understand me!"

Evan turned to look over his shoulder, "Yes, sir. We understand." The old man from the restaurant the other night stood back about five feet. He was wearing the same striped shirt as before as if this was his costume for his role as the salty sea-dog at the local community theater. However, this didn't feel much like a play now. The gun he was holding in his hand definitely seemed real. Evan could see he was holding a set of boat keys in his other hand, the fluorescent orange float dangling in the dark by his side.

"I didn't say turn around. I asked if you understand." He took a step closer, cutting the distance between them by half, and centered the gun on Evan's face. "I didn't say look at me. You're off to a bad start, hotshot."

Evan quickly turned back around. He felt Ross' shaking hand. "Evan, just do what he says. Please," he silently implored. His brother seemed small beside him.

Evan's thoughts flashed to the time they were separated from their parents in the Prague metro station. His mom and dad had been working on an article about the Prague Castle, and the family was returning to their hotel room to put away their bags and change before grabbing dinner later that evening. His parents' hands were full with the many lenses, rolls of film and cameras his dad had brought to take pictures that day, so the boys were told to stay close and stay together while traveling through the bustling city. Ross, who couldn't have been more than eight at the time, clung to Evan's hand obediently, and Evan remembered feeling encumbered by his little brother. The crowd who was waiting on the platform to board the approaching train had grown so large with busy commuters. It felt like being surrounded by a swarm of bees, and the brothers were pushed back, unable to get on board before the doors automatically closed. By the time their parents turned to see the boys still standing on the platform separated from them by sealed glass doors, the train was pulling away. Left alone in a now empty station, Ross looked up at Evan, his eyes welling with tears, pleading for help. "What are we going to do?"

Ross was looking at Evan now, with those same eyes that were filling with tears, looking to his brother to figure a way out of this mess. Evan felt the same panic now that he had in Prague. He was scared for himself, of course, but that fear was magnified by his need to protect his brother and Maera.

However, he could not allow his fear to settle within him. It was his job to be the strong one. Ross needed him. Maera needed him.

"Now, I'm gonna say this again only one time. You do exactly what I say and nothing else. Got that? That way nobody gets hurt. Do you understand me?" He was speaking to them loudly and slowly, drawing out each word, as if they were hard of hearing or stupid. Evan thought the man's southern accent would be comical, had the situation been different.

"Yes. We got that." Evan tried to keep his voice from wavering. He didn't want Ross to know he was terrified. He didn't want Maera to feel any more scared than she already was, but he did want her to know that he was there. He centered his thoughts and gaze directly at her, "I'm here, Maera. You're going to be just fine. I'll get you out of there. I promise. I have the key." He could see her body shift on the bed inside.

"Oh Evan. Please be careful. Please!"

"I will. Everything is going to be ok."

Being near her made him feel stronger and calmer. He was beginning to believe his own promises. He had already found the key. He would find a way out of this too.

In Prague, he had remained calm and found a station agent who radioed ahead to the next station. They waited with him for just a short time while their parents were contacted and then returned on the next train. No station agents were around who could radio for help now, but Evan knew that if he remained calm, the solution would reveal itself. Remain calm, remain calm, he repeated to himself several times. He knew he could. He knew he had to, for Maera and for Ross.

"Ok, hotshot. I'm glad you understand. What about your boy here? Do you also understand, my friend?"

"He's a mute, sir. He can't talk." Evan blurted out before Ross had a chance to respond.

"Evan...," he heard Ross pleading in his mind.

"Well is he deaf and dumb too? Can he understand me?"

"Oh, yes sir, he can hear you just fine. There's nothing wrong with his brain." Evan could see Ross vigorously nodding in the affirmative next to him. "He just can't talk, sir. Even if he wanted to." Evan knew this was a lie but figured it was better than trying to explain his brother's peculiar penchant for silence.

"Well, good, then. That will make things simpler. Only one of you to keep quiet. Now, what have you boys done with my key? Oh, and did you see my glowing treasure inside? Quite a find! I mean, to find the Mermaid's Key was thrilling enough, but to have it in combination with that beautiful creature... Hot damn! I've hit the jackpot. " The old man's laugh sounded like that of a sinister villain from the old movies until it died into a choking cough. Evan could hear him coarsely hawk a glob of dense wet substance to the decking beside them.

The man repulsed him, and Evan felt his spine snap straight with fury. He clenched his fists, tightening his grip on Ross' hand even more. How did this guy know the significance of the key? How did he know that it was the property of merpeople? What were his plans for Maera? A flame of heat surged up from his core and scorched Ross through their gripped hands.

"Evan, please don't do anything stupid. Let's think this through before you act impulsively. He's just trying to goad you. Please..." Ross sounded terrified and small, like the little boy in the Prague train station.

Evan knew Ross was right. "It's ok." He took a deep breath of the cooling night air to squelch his rage. "You're right. We'll figure this out." Trying to sound reassuring and strong for both his brother and Maera, who he knew was still listening. "I'm thinking we've got several options," but before he could continue, he felt the cold metal of the gun jab at his shoulder.

"What's with all the pansy hand-holding? Knock it off, and get on board," the man said, as he shoved at Evan.

"Sir, my brother's really scared. That's all. Just let me..."

"Hotshot, I don't know how long it's gonna take for you to figure out this isn't a game. The rules are simple. I'm the one with the gun. You do what I say, when I say!" demanded the man in a louder and sharper tone.

Evan could feel Ross trying to release his grip, but he held firm. "Evan, just do what he says. Let go of me," Ross begged in his mind.

"No, Ross. If we're gonna figure this out, we need to stay connected." Evan tightened his grip on Ross' hand. He started to reply to the man, "Sir, I understand, but..."

Evan felt a crack, and an explosion of heat at the side of his head as the man smacked him hard with the butt of the gun. He heard both Ross and Maera call out his name, but they sounded far away. His knees buckled and like a building imploding during a demolition and he felt himself cave inward. Then, it was dark.

Chapter 17

Pins of light were all he could see. Evan blinked several times, trying to clear his vision. His head pounded so loudly that all he could hear was each pulse of his heart, making a whooshing sound, like the spinning blade of a turbine engine. He was enclosed in heat and dampness with the choking smell of mildew. His exhalations remained close to his face, trapped by the cloth that cloaked his head. Jammed into a tight space, unable to straighten his back or legs, he turned his head from side to side trying to locate where he was, but he was unable to shake the cover from his eyes. He tried to reach up but found that his hands were bound behind his back. The harder he pulled, the tighter the sharp cord became around his wrists, biting deeper into his skin. His breath quickened, and that only made it harder to breathe. Then, he heard her.

"It's ok, Evan. I'm right here." He felt her finger brush the tip of his, and their current again flowed. Warmth and light surged from her to him. It softened the rigid fear that gripped him. Maera. Her name played like a song in his mind.

And then he remembered. The old man, the boat, the key, Maera bound and blindfolded, the whack to the back of his head. That was it. He must be inside the boat beside Maera. The points of light in his vision and the dank closeness. He also had a pillowcase over his head now. Luckily, he could still feel the device slightly pulsing at his temple, so he could still hear Maera's thoughts inside his head, but where was Ross? A new wave of terror surged inside him.

"I don't know where he took Ross," he heard Maera answer in his mind. While he was reassured by the presence of her beside him, it was not enough to control the panic that rippled through him. The old man could have taken Ross anywhere. Ross could be hurt or worse.

Unable to continue with worries of the unknown, he shifted his focus to questions he knew could be answered. "How long have I been out? Are we still on that guys' boat? How long have they been gone?" His head pounded harder as his thoughts pinged around like a pinball machine. The knot on the back of his head pressed against the mattress edge. He shifted his position to help ease the pain, but this caused the cord around his wrists to bind tighter. He struggled to remain still.

The springs of the mattress groaned as she stretched toward him. Two fingertips now met his. Their strengthening connection calmed him. "You've been out for a while, but I'm not sure for how long. I was beginning to worry that he might have done more than just knock you out, so I counted your breathing to make sure you were still with me. I willed it to continue. I've been counting for a long time. I was about to hit 2,000."

"What?" Evan struggled to quickly multiply the numbers. "That's like 30 minutes! He could have taken Ross anywhere in that amount of time." A wave of panic surged, and he thought he was going to throw up again. His stomach clenched and heaved, but nothing came. For the first time today, he was thankful his stomach was empty. He could only imagine how horrible filling the pillowcase with puke might be.

Maera's fingers were stretched as far as they could, and yet only the two could reach his. She struggled to connect more. "I was able to get one hand free, but I'm still tied to the desk by the other arm. I can't get my other hand out and can't untie the knot that's holding the sack over my head with only one hand. Every time I pull, the binding on my arm gets tighter. I can't reach any further." She was rambling with worry, but paused before adding, "I want to hold you."

I want to hold you. Those five simple words were the most beautiful Evan had ever heard, rather felt, from another person. It awakened in him a charge - a hypnotic pull. The force was so strong, like his insides might rip from within and defy his bound body, so that he could reach her. As he struggled towards her, the plastic tie on his wrists sliced the outer edges. He felt a small drop of warm liquid fall onto the back of his shirt and assumed he was bleeding. The old guy must have used zip-ties to bind their wrists. The cuts burned, but the desire still pulled him to her. "I want to hold you," he offered back to her. He marveled at how, in this horrible place, blindfolded and tied up, with the stench of a rotting alligator carcass pressing into the room through the thin ceiling, and his brother in certain danger, that he could feel himself falling so deeply in love with this girl from another world. Surely, at some point, this dream would have to end.

"I know. I keep thinking that I'll wake up eventually," Maera responded. "But then again, I keep hoping that the dream will continue. Because if it were to end, I would lose you, and I can't bear that thought." Surprising Evan, she giggled. "So somehow, in some strange way, I'm thankful I'm here."

Evan laughed at her absurd thought but also found himself in agreement. Her thoughts were so fortifying, filling Evan with confidence. "I couldn't agree more." Evan paused for a deep breath to refocus. "As great as this may seem, we've got to find a way out of here, and save Ross. Did you hear them say anything before they left?"

"Well, the old guy was shouting at Ross, but since I can't understand him without the communicator, I had no idea what he was saying. He was just so loud and scary." Evan could feel her shudder. "After tossing you down beside me and tying you up, he rummaged around this place, screaming all the while. I was terrified, but Ross was so calm and kind through it all. He kept trying to reassure me that everything would be ok. He wasn't talking to the guy, though. He didn't say one word out loud. He told me that he was going to mislead the guy by writing something down."

She paused as if distracted. "It's really strange, and I still can't figure it out. I have no idea how Ross and I can communicate. It doesn't make sense that he can do it without the device." Evan heard her exhale and thought he could feel her shake the confusion from her head before continuing.

"But anyway, I could picture what Ross was writing. He wrote 'HOTEL ROOM' on a slip of paper and gave it to the old man. There was some more commotion and yelling, and then they were gone. I called after Ross, but he was too far away to feel his response. I don't know for sure, but I guess maybe the old guy took Ross back to the hotel room, thinking he would find the key there." Maera paused for a beat before asking, "You still have the key, right?"

Evan could feel the weight and coolness of the key pressing against his thigh. It was still in the pockets of his shorts which remained damp from swimming not long ago. "Yes, of course. I promised you I would get it." Evan felt himself beam at his success. He was bolstered by it as well and added, "I promised to get you out of here also, and I will."

"I know you will."

Her confidence in him made him feel even stronger and more focused. "Ok, let's think. We know Ross is no dummy. I bet he thought we were in way over our heads and needed our parents' help. I'm sure either our Mom or Dad has been in the hotel room all day waiting for us to come back. They probably even have the police involved by now. Ross would know that and would want to lead the old guy back there. That guy was desperate to get the key back, and I'm positive Ross told him we took the key back to our hotel room so that he could get help."

Evan was beginning to feel like he had the upper hand on his emotions for the first time today. His breathing was normal, and his brain felt clear. This must be how Ross feels all the time and why he's able to solve problems so quickly. He went on, "So if Ross was able to lead the guy back to our parents and/or the police, he must be safe. Let's hope he is, at least." Evan felt hopeful. The urgency to find Ross diminished slightly. He refused to entertain the possibility that maybe Ross hadn't made it to their parents or that they were in danger now as well. "If he's safe, then perhaps everyone is on their way back here to rescue us."

Alarm coursed through Maera. "But everyone can't come here and find me! I'm not one of you. I glow, remember!" Her breathing was quick and shallow.

Before being knocked out, Evan had only begun to imagine what the old guy had planned for Maera. If he had a rotting alligator on his roof, Evan didn't want to think about what this guy was capable of. He had not had the chance to consider what might happen if his parents, or worse, the police, discovered Maera. She was alien in this world. Would his parents allow her to be taken away for studies and testing like they had planned to do with the key? Surely not, he hoped. She was human, after all, not some artifact to be examined. Likely, they would send her back to her world with some typical explanation that it would be for the best. The image of his little salamander friend placed beside the cool water of the mountain stream flickered in his mind. He recalled the crushing feeling of sadness that his little boy self had felt as he walked away, leaving it behind. He couldn't fathom how great the pain would be if they sent Maera home and asked him to walk away from her now. He wouldn't let that happen.

"I know, I know. It's ok. We can figure this out." Evan's fingertips pressed firmly against Maera's, and he heard her breathing slowly somewhat. "We just have to find a way out of these blindfolds and ties. We can do that. We have the key, and we've still got the kayaks. So we can paddle back to the island, and you can get back unseen." Evan felt himself sinking again at the thought of Maera returning. This was the part of the plan he wasn't prepared for. The part that made the reality of it all too much.

"Come with me!" Maera blurted out. "I mean, I know, it's crazy. I haven't figured it all out yet but just come with me. I...you..."

Evan could feel her struggling for what came next. He didn't know either. He'd be as much an alien in her world as she was in his. No matter from which direction you came at it, the result was still the same. They didn't have a place in each other's universe.

"We can worry about that part later," he said, wanting to pause her thoughts as well as his. He couldn't deal with that now. He wasn't sure that he could even deal with that later. "Right now, all we have to do is get out of here."

He tried to focus his view through the small holes of the pillowcase fabric but could barely make out the details of the room around him. While he couldn't see much, he remembered the simple layout from before and knew there had been a knife on the counter. He had seen it sitting on the cutting board next to the picked-over fish carcass. It was not far from where Maera was lying now. "Can you reach behind you with your arm?"

"Yeah, with this one." He felt her touch against his fingertips again. Another pulse of energy flowed. He knew he would never tire of that sensation.

"Awesome. So there's a counter behind you, over your right shoulder." Maera's touch left him, and he heard her free arm strike the counter with force, spilling dishes on the floor. A glass broke.

"Ow." He heard her suck in air through her teeth. "It's closer behind me than I thought. Aaah," she sighed.

"Are you ok?" Evan tried to reach out to her, but the binding cut deeper into his wrist, and he grunted in pain.

"Yeah, are you?" Maera replied with concern.

"I'm fine. I just keep forgetting I'm tied up, and every time I pull against it, the binding gets tighter." Evan could feel more warm blood dripping from a cut in his wrist but refocused his attention to the plan. "Ok, so now that you know where it is, feel along the edge of the counter. It's not very big. There should be a sink with a bunch of dishes in it." He heard clanking as she moved her hand along.

"Ugh, I stuck my hand in something slimy."

"Yeah, this guy's a slob. Sorry." Evan wished he could be more of a help.

"I know. What's that terrible smell, anyway?" Evan was sure she was referring to the stench of the alligator that was seeping into the room, but he didn't have time to reply before Maera continued, "Nevermind. What am I looking for?"

Evan smiled at how determined and capable she was. "A knife. I know there was one on the counter earlier. If you can feel around to the left of the sink, there should be a small counter space with a cutting board and knife." He waited as he heard her moving her hand around.

"I feel the board, but there's nothing on it but scales, bones and ugh, dampness, like leftover food. Are you sure there's a knife up here."

"I don't know. There was. Maybe he took it with him, so we wouldn't be able to cut ourselves free."

"Well..." she paused as her hand stilled rummaged around on the counter. "I don't think the knife is here." But before Evan's hope dimmed, she persisted, "Ah, I know. I just broke that glass. I can use that. Hold on." He felt Maera shifting her position on the mattress and again heard her suck air across her teeth. "Well, I found the glass."

"Did you cut yourself?" Evan wished there was something more he could do. He felt so helpless lying there.

"Yeah, but it's not bad, just a nick. I'm fine." The bed shifted again, and he heard Maera groan quietly as she struggled to cut her other arm free. Minutes passed while she worked at the thick plastic zip-tie. Her attention was so intently focused on her work that Evan couldn't hear her in his thoughts. He found himself holding his breath until finally, he heard her say, "I've got it!"

The mattress springs creaked as Maera sat up. After another few moments of her struggling with the knot that secured the cloth on her head, he heard her breathe a loud sigh of relief when she finally removed the pillowcase. Evan's body rocked with the changing weight on the bed. He felt her warm body lean across his to reach his hands behind him. With only two quick slices, his wrists were free. Blood rushed back into his hands and pricked like a hundred biting ants. He hadn't realized how impaired his circulation had become by the tightening binds. She fiddled with the knot on his blindfold for only a moment. When she pulled the sack from his head, the light blinded him, but he welcomed the coolness of the air. He took a deep breath, brought his hands to his face, and rubbed hard.

When he opened his eyes, Maera was there before him, her face only inches from his. A halo of light glowed behind her like an aura. Evan couldn't decide if it was his imagination, his eyes adjusting to the intensity of the single bare bulb illuminating the room after being cloaked in darkness or her natural luminosity, but before he could decide, she leaned in and placed her mouth on his. He closed his eyes and felt himself melt into her. Less hurried and surprising than their first kiss and certainly less awkward than their second, he had time to enjoy her now. He felt her smiling, knowing that she shared his memory as well.

His hands reached behind her and pulled her closer. She pressed on top of him, and he held her there as the kiss deepened. One hand tightened around her waist, and the other moved up behind her head into her strands of silken hair. A moan of pleasure escaped her and encouraged him to kiss harder, their mouths opening. All of his senses became so filled that he felt drunk on her. They both pulled away, breathless, but their eyes remained locked on each other.

"Oh my," Evan said in a hush.

Chapter 18

Unable to think and unwilling to leave this moment, Evan's hand traced the side of Maera's cheek. The smile in her eyes dimmed when she reminded him, "We have to go."

"I know. I just wish we could pause right here for a while." As he looked around the small filthy room, he corrected himself. "Well, not here, exactly."

She giggled, "I know exactly what you mean, but seriously, we have to go now." She pulled away from him and sat up on the bed beside him.

Evan sat up as well and pushed his hair back and down, trying to control his wild mop. "You're right. I guess we should get to the kayaks," but the mere suggestion of them reawakened the ache in his shoulders and arms. "Ugh, I'm not looking forward to paddling for a fourth time today. I wish there was another way."

"I know, I do too." She reached out and began to massage his right shoulder and arm, somehow knowing the exact spot of his most intense discomfort. In addition to knowing his thoughts, she seemed intuitive to his feelings as well. "But it's what we have to do. I have to get the key back. And the longer we stay here, the bigger the risk. That guy might come back, or your parents. I can't be discovered. I, I..." she paused, not wanting to admit the rest, "I don't belong here." She cast her eyes downward and pulled her hand away.

Evan wanted desperately to convince her that there was another way, but he knew she was right. His gaze fell too, and he saw the outline of the key in his pocket. He removed it and turned it in his hand several times, tracing the edges and curves. When he had first found this key, he had wondered what door it might unlock. Never in a million years would he have imagined it would lead him to Maera. He remembered the story she told him about the key when they met last night. That seemed so long ago now. So much had happened since then. The myth that the key would unlock one's whole self, that it might lead to "the way." As he stroked the smooth opalescent stones wrapped by the metal of the key, he couldn't help but think that it had. He looked up and met Maera's cool blue gaze.

Her hands reached out for his, and they cradled the key between them. "I know. I have never believed any of those stories. I've always felt so isolated from the beliefs of my people. I mean, my mom is the leader of it all, the top priestess, and the key has been her life's work. No matter how many times she has explained its significance or how many arguments we've had, I've never been able to reconcile how a piece of metal could have any power." She swallowed hard before continuing, "But, it's all been true. The key led me to you."

Evan's mind was staggering with the weight of it all. Within the span of 24 hours, he had found a mysterious key that led him to the girl who was the yin to his yang. It was like somehow the universe had a hand in pulling them from opposite worlds, so they might find each other. Had it not actually been happening to him, he would have found it too corny an idea to entertain. He had always dismissed the fairy tales and love stories about meeting "the one" and clearly, so had Maera. He had scoffed at the notion of love at first sight, but he couldn't dismiss it now that he felt it was happening to him.

The bubble in which Evan and Maera had just been floating was instantly popped when the boat's screen door swung open with a loud creak. Evan and Maera had barely jumped to their feet before the old guy blocked the exit. With a gun still in hand and a sour smirk across his face, he chuckled, "Ah, I see you had my key after all." He alternated between pointing the gun at Maera and Evan.

He scowled at their untied wrists. "Did you think you were going somewhere? Were the blindfolds and ties not indication enough that you were supposed to wait for me to come back? I distinctly remember telling you both to stay put."

The old man's face was flushed, and he paused, trying to catch his breath. It seemed that he may have just been running in order to rush back here. He loudly exhaled before stepping inside the room. "Your stupid brother thought he could trick me by leading me back to the hotel room." He moved towards the sink, still keeping the gun pointed at them, and pulled a can of beer from a small refrigerator below the counter. He popped the top of the can and took a long drink. He emitted a foul, wet burp before continuing. "But there was no key there, just some woman, even more foolish than your brother, who thought she'd be able to stop me."

"Mom!" Evan couldn't help but blurt out.

"Yeah, I figured as much." He rolled his eyes dismissively. "But I didn't spend much time chatting it up with her. Once I realized the key wasn't there, I gave the two of them a quick whap to the head and headed back here. I knew you had it."

Evan felt his insides clench with equal parts rage and terror. His breathing was becoming rapid. Maera's hand wrapped around his, the key pressing between their palms. The current again swelled between them. "What's happening? What's he saying? And what is he pointing at us? It looks dangerous."

"The gun? It's... it's..." He couldn't think of the words necessary to explain how a gun worked and certainly didn't want to think about what it could do. "Yeah, it's very dangerous." Evan desperately wanted to tell her everything would be all right, that he could handle this, but his mind was a swirling eddy of fears - his mom and Ross could be hurt, or worse, there was a gun pointed at Maera and him, and after all they had been through, they were going to lose the key. He squeezed Maera's hand tighter, hoping that may convince her, and more so himself, that they could handle this.

"What's with you and all the hand holding, hot shot? I swear, it's just plain weird." The old man took another swig of beer. He wiped the back of his hand across his lips and belched again loudly.

Evan figured he had nothing to lose, so he jumped to his feet and fired back. "Oh, yeah. What's it to you?" He was embarrassed that he wasn't able to come up with anything better than this childish retort and scrambled to gain some sort of upper hand in the conversation. "Really, what is it to you? Why do you want this worthless key anyway? You're really going to risk going to jail for kidnapping and assault over some trinket?" He knew it was a stretch, but he had to try something.

The old man drank another gulp of beer during Evan's outburst, showing that he obviously was not ruffled by some teenage boy's meager attempt at brashness. At the word trinket, he choked on his drink as he tried to suppress his laugh. He pulled the can from his mouth and forced a swallow before responding as he chuckled. "Boy, do you think I'm stupid or something?" Drops of yellow beer clung to his white beard as he continued, "You and I both know that key is no trinket." Turning towards Maera seated on the bed, he directed his question to her. "Am I right about that little miss?"

Maera couldn't hold the man's gaze and looked down at her feet. Evan felt her begin to shake through the hand he still held. "Stop scaring her," Evan shouted back. "She can't understand you." Evan was shaking too and hoped it wasn't visible.

"That's 'cause she's a mermaid, isn't it? Not only do I have the sacred key, which is worth millions by the way, but I've got this sweet little… what would you call her? A trinket?" He laughed at his own joke. "I've got my own sweet little trinket to go along with the key. I've found the treasure of a lifetime." He laughed fuller now, making Evan's skin crawl. "No more scanning the bottom of the ocean for shipwrecks. No more selling exotic animals and skins."

So that explains the gator rotting on the roof, thought Evan.

The old man continued. "No more living on this hunk of garbage. No sir, I've got me a rarefied mermaid along with the most valued of all mermaid treasures."

"How do you know about the key?" Evan pushed back.

"Really, son? The question is… how do you know about the key? How did you come to find yourself in possession of the key and in the company of this siren?"

A brief laugh burst forth from Evan, surprising everyone in the room. The old man's questions were the exact ones he had been asking himself for the past two days. How did this key wash up on the same beach on which Evan found himself aimlessly walking? How did Maera appear before him last night on the island his family was never meant to sleep on? "Fate," Evan responded with boldness. It seemed to be the only answer he could supply.

"Ah, fate." The old man pulled the words out slow and long. "So it seems the myth of the key is true. Excellent. That only enhances the worth."

"How do you…" Evan struggled to formulate a question when he had so many. "Who are you going to sell the key to anyway?" He also wanted to know what he planned on doing with Maera, but he didn't have the courage to hear that answer.

"Boy," the vowel sound stretched so long it gave the word two syllables. "Any true sailor out there knows about the legend of this key and the mermaids that go with it. Some men spend their whole lives searching for treasures such as these. Have you never heard of pirates?" He laughed, and his large belly jiggled. He was obviously having fun with this. "I know ten men I could sell the key to today. I'm actually anticipating a bidding war." The man's eyes sparkled as if reflecting off the piles of gold he was imaging he would earn from its sale.

He paused and stroked his beard in contemplation. "But what to do with her is the real question?" He looked Maera up and down several times, licking his lips as he did so. Evan seethed. "I'm awfully disappointment she doesn't have a tail." The old man cocked his head to the side and raised one eyebrow in further contemplation. "However, the glowing bit is a nice surprise." He took a step forward and reached to stroke the side of Maera's cheek. "She's quite a prize, alright," he added in a tone that made Maera's skin visibly crawl and caused her to recoil. Regardless of the language barrier, she clearly understood the sentiment.

Like a bolt of lightning, and without conscious intent, Evan struck out against the man, shoving him back with two hands. Had there been more space behind him, the old guy would have fallen from the force, but he was able to catch himself on the counter and recover quickly with a stagger.

"Ah, come on," he growled. "You almost made me drop the rest of my beer." The man finished the drink in one last pull and crushed the empty can while refocusing his gaze and gun at Evan. "I'm done with this question and answer." He centered the gun at Evan's face and tightened his tone to a forceful bark. "Sit down, son. I have the gun. I win. It's as simple as that, you fool." His upper teeth scraped against his beer-soaked lower lip as he forcefully spoke the last word, and a fleck of spit sprayed from his mouth, hitting Evan in the face.

Evan brazenly wiped away the warm drop that had struck his cheek, but his boldness was quickly replaced by returning fear. Trembling from the after-effects of his rage, and due to the gun that was just inches from his face, Evan took a step back and sat down slowly next to Maera on the edge of the bed. Her hand quickly scrambled to grasp his. "Evan..." she pleaded in small voice.

The old man tossed the crushed can half-heartedly in the direction of the sink. It missed and bounced into the corner, landing atop a dirty sock. With the gun still pointed on Evan, his face tightened with disappointment. "Oh, and I don't like that you lied to me either. That pansy brother of yours isn't a mute, and you know it. The moment we got back to that hotel room, he was all like 'Mom, mom, Evan's in trouble... he's tied up on this crazy man's boat, blah, blah, blah...'" The old man's voice squeaked in a whiny, inaccurate reproduction of Ross' tone. He continued in his own gravelly drawl. "In fact, the only way I could get him to stop blabbing was to knock him upside the head."

Evan closed his eyes and bit his lip thinking of Ross lying passed out on the floor of the hotel room. He was touched that Ross had broken his vow and spoke because of him. He had done his best to save him. Evan's stomach pulled the tightest it had all day as if it were turning itself inside-out deep inside him.

He had to lower his head between his knees to keep himself from passing out. The image of the gun cracking against Ross' head rolled inside a barrelling wave of emotion. Another wave crashed onto him as the image of his mom being struck by the gun piled into his surging mind. He felt like he might be drowned by his thoughts, unable to pull himself above the swirling torrent of water - a Charybdis inside. He couldn't hold back any longer, and he wretched again. This time it was only clear liquid since his stomach was now completely devoid of anything else.

"Damn it all to hell, boy!" the man yelled. "You've stolen my key, shoved me, lied to me, and now puked on my floor." He shook his head, disgusted by the mess and let out a heavy breath. "You sure do seem like under different circumstances you might be a nice enough kid. But really, this is just too much. It's gone on too long." Using the gun as an extension of his hand, he wagged it at Evan, as if trying to explain his point. "But really, it's a shame I have to get rid of you."

Evan slowly lifted his head from between his knees, so his gaze could meet the old man's. He didn't even have it in him to plead. He was empty... completely... all wrung out. His hand still held to Maera's, but he couldn't hear her thoughts as he had before. Now it was something more. He could feel them instead. He could feel her rage at the old man. She burned hot, as hot as any rage within him had ever burned. Her anger was so big it rippled from her like heat waves across the desert. Her fury was so strong it spilled out of her and into him, spreading like a forest fire. While before he was empty, he now felt himself filling with her overflow. The void inside him was replaced by a flame that grew strong enough to extinguish the waves of dread and fear that threatened to drown him before. While all this transpired, he didn't take his eyes off the old man. Once his rage burned as hot as hers, Evan spit the remaining bile from his mouth, and it struck the old man's face.

As if struck by a hot coal that bounced out of the fire, the old man took a step back in shock. Maera didn't waste a moment to exploit his distraction and lunged at his knees, knocking him off balance and to the floor. Stunned only for a second by her boldness, Evan couldn't help but smile at Maera. Beautiful, bold, and strong...Evan knew he was completely hooked by her now. Less bewitched by the moment than he was, Maera turned to Evan with a look on her face that needed no communicator device to decode. It seemed to scream at him - "What are you waiting for? Come on!"

Evan jumped to his feet and kicked the gun free from the old man's hand as he still lay stunned on the ground, unable to recover from Maera's blow. It was like kicking a hornet's nest because the old man growled and came to life with a fury all his own. Maera had turned and begun to head for the door. Before she could reach it, the old man had pulled his body halfway up, enough so that he could grab her by the hair. The sound of Maera's scream tore through Evan's ears, filling him with even more strength. He grabbed for the old man's hair in repayment, and while holding firmly to the greasy strands with both hands, he slammed the man's face against the side of the cabinets.

The old man released Maera and came at Evan with full vengeance. With one quick movement, his right arm flung around, hooking Evan in the chest and thrusting back hard. The corner of the desk met Evan's back with such force that it felt as if his left kidney had exploded. Winded and struggling to right himself, Evan only had time to cover his head with both hands as he saw the old man rise up above him, poised to strike. Anticipating the blow, Evan closed his eyes. He heard a whack but felt no pain.

Scared of what he might find, he opened his eyes slowly and saw the old man crumpled on the ground before him. Maera was standing behind the man's deflated body. She was breathing hard and holding the gun upside down with both hands, which were lowering from their raised position above her head. As if it were suddenly hot in her hands, she dropped the gun to the floor and turned her attention from the man to Evan. The fierce iciness in her eyes melted, returning to their cool radiant blue. She knelt before him and touched his face with her hand. "Are you ok?" she asked, her eyebrows knitted with worry.

Evan's breathing felt labored. "I think so." As he stood, he flinched from the pain that clamped onto the left side of his back. Rubbing the spot with his hand, he straightened his body and replied, "Yeah, I'm fine. Are you?" He carefully stepped over the man's body and reached his arms around Maera.

Breathing hard, she leaned into Evan, allowing him to envelop her. She buried her face into his chest and replied, "Yes, I am, now." Pausing to enjoy the embrace for only a moment, she pulled back and looked pleadingly into his face. "But we have to get out of here. This guy is clearly dangerous, and we have no idea how long he is going to remain out. I really think he meant to kill you, Evan. I was so scared!"

Evan swallowed the lump in his throat, struggling to suppress the horror of the night's events. Maera's kidnapping, being held at gunpoint, his mom and Ross lying unconscious on the hotel room floor. He didn't want to think about that man's intentions any longer and certainly did not want to wait around for him to wake up either. Leading her out the door, Evan turned to look back at her and nodded. "I know he did." Pulling Maera up and out of the houseboat, he continued, "but, if that's how you act when you're scared, I'd hate to see you mad." He teased recalling the ferocity with which Maera had attacked. She closed her mouth over her teeth trying to conceal her smile, but couldn't hide the twinkling in her eyes as she beamed back at Evan, obviously proud of herself. Squeezing her hand affectionately, Evan continued, "You should be really proud of yourself. You're the reason we're out of there, safe now." He held the screen door open for her to step off the boat. "Ladies first."

Maera chuckled as she nodded and stepped past. "What's so funny?" Evan wondered.

Continuing down the dock to put as much room between them and the old man, as quickly as possible, Maera explained. "It's just so strange, your world, that is. It's such a paradox to mine. While you have 'ladies first,' we have 'men, if you please.'" She laughed again, thinking about it. "As a girl, I'd always resented the absurdity of having to let the boys go first. When I would question my mom about the custom, she'd simply respond, 'It's just polite, that's all.'"

Evan snickered at a similar memory of when he had been taught to hold a door open for women. He had remembered wondering that if women are equal to men, why was he expected to behave otherwise? Not that he thought the women's liberation movement made it so he didn't have to be polite to women. He just didn't understand the outdated custom that suggested they were somehow weaker. Clearly, it didn't stop him from applying it with Maera just now. He supposed he had been hoping to impress her by holding the door for her.

Maera continued, "I'd never considered the existence of the converse, but here it is."

"Yin and yang," Evan posited as he quickened his pace to keep up with Maera on the dock. He had been thinking about its significance all day and was reminded of it again.

"What's that? I've seen that black and white circular symbol flash in your thoughts several times before, and I was wondering what it meant. Yin and yang, you called it?" Evan could see Maera's questioning expression against the dark night. Her soft blue glow pulsed rapidly. Evan assumed it was from the exertion of their pace since they were practically running down the dock.

"Um, yeah…" Evan paused to collect his thoughts, made uneasy by the reminder that she had full access to the inventory of his brain but also in order to make sure he could correctly remember which was which. Yin was the black one, right? He figured it didn't exactly matter right now and proceeded with his explanation. " It's this theory about how opposites are actually complement each other." He clearly pictured the image of white twisting into the black of a circle and felt it pass from his mind to hers. She nodded with understanding. "Both sides are chasing after each other as they seek balance within the other." His fingers intertwined with hers. He smiled, thinking of the two of them - complements.

"Ah, like us," she responded with a squeeze. "And our myth of the key." Evan's heart skipped as he worried they had forgotten to retrieve the key in the preceding commotion, but he quickly was relieved when Maera pulled the key from the pocket of Ross' shirt that she was still wearing. Both paused their hurried retreat, and she held it between them to examine. "This key is the symbol of unlocking our complementary connection. The tines of the key fit only into their exact negative space." The fingers on her hand slid out from between Evan's, paused, and then slid back into place among his. "And by doing so, unlock the mystery... you become complete. Balanced."

Remembering that they were standing on the dock in the middle of the marina, Evan urged. "We have to keep moving."

Unmoved, Maera was looking down at their connected hands. "But I don't know what to do." She lifted her eyes to meet his. Worry pulled her brows together as she searched Evan for the answer. "I can't go, and I can't stay."

Evan knew exactly what she meant. He had been putting off the inevitability of this conundrum all day, shooing the Catch-22 from his mind, pushing away the worry until later. It had worked so far, so he suggested it again now. "Well, we can't stand here and discuss it, that's for sure. That guy is bound to wake up sooner or later, and we can't be anywhere near him when he does. Let's at least head back to the kayaks, and get out of the marina before we make any decisions. How does that sound?"

Maera bit her lower lip and shifted her eyes to the side as if she was trying to hold back tears. Evan bit down on the edges of his tongue to avoid the same in response. The sadness of her face pulled at him. He wanted to provide an immediate solution, rescue her from her predicament, but what he had just suggested was all he could offer. "We can think as we paddle out of here and reconnect then. I'll give you some space to deliberate." As much as he didn't want to admit it, he added, " I think I could use some mental space myself."

Thinking back over the day, he realized that he had someone in his mind since Ross arrived on the beach this afternoon. He was exhausted. Not only had the physical and emotional exertion of the day's events taxed him, he wasn't used to sharing his mind with others. The idea of not having a way to communicate with Maera, if only for a short time, made him feel desirous. His want of her was outweighed now by his need to have some time for his own thoughts only.

"That doesn't hurt your feelings, does it?" The question made Evan realize that while he felt completely connected with Maera, he still didn't know her preferences or sensitivities.

"No, of course not," she assured. "I think you're right. We both need some time to process everything that has happened today and consider some very difficult choices regarding how we proceed. Let's get the kayaks, and get back to the island before we decide anything else. During that time, let's just think. Alone." She squeezed his hand tightly and nodded with certainty.

Then without waiting for any further discussion on the matter, she reached up and removed the pulsing orb from Evan's temple. Evan felt like he was going off the grid. While the sound was the simple slurp of a brief breaking of the suction, in Evan's mind, it sounded like the power going out over a whole city. It was like the descending sound of a huge motor being powered down. Dizziness overtook him again, and he staggered to keep his balance. Maera's hand reached out to support his elbow. Her eyes asked if he was all right, but her voice did not accompany the question in his mind. Their connection was now only physical, no longer mental. He could still feel her electrical current pulse through him, but no more radio connection - no more mental chatter. Struggling to adjust to the change in sensation, he nodded to reassure her he was fine, gave a feeble smile, and turned in the direction of the kayaks. While he had been the one who suggested the time to think, he missed her already.

Chapter 19

Without someone else's thoughts streaming through, Evan felt like a vast canyon had opened in his mind. He no longer had Maera echoing back, responding to his ideas. His thinking was allowed to simply stream into the void. It was comforting and lonely all at the same time.

They continued to walk quickly, now silently, back to where the kayaks were stashed. He lowered himself down into the one boat, but before he could turn to help her, Maera was situating herself in the other. He raised his paddle and looked to her to ask if she knew how, and she nodded and began paddling toward the entrance of the marina. She moved through the water with such confidence and ease, it seemed she had been doing it her entire life. Evan marveled at her natural abilities and tried to picture himself in the reverse. If marooned in her world, would he just as easily take to swimming through the depths with one of those breathing masks she had shown him in her mind the night before? Were they really that different after all, he wondered? He paddled stronger to keep up.

The night was darker now, as clouds began to fill the sky, covering the moon and stars. This amplified her glow, making Evan nervous that she would be spotted while paddling out of the marina into the open water of the Gulf. Perhaps they were more different than he wanted to believe. She could never fit in here. She would never be safe.

He then realized the converse for him in her world might also be true. Would the fact that he did not glow stand out there as starkly as her glowing did here? Perhaps it was just as simple as diet modification, he countered within himself. She had said the reason she glowed was because of something she ate. If he went with her and began eating the way she did, would he glow too? He thought that was how it worked in other bioluminescent animals, but then again, did it matter whether he glowed? Maybe her people were less violent or more accepting?

Yet he knew the real question was not could they live in each other's worlds. Could they leave their own behind? Evan had never felt like he belonged, he knew that. He had no real friends, aside from Ross and his parents. He loved his family and knew without a doubt they loved him, but he also knew he had never really been one of them. Ross and his parents had this exquisite peace about them. They had discipline. They were kind and gentle. They didn't have the same fire that burned inside Evan, the temper and passion. He was different and always had been. Was that enough to make him leave and perhaps never see them again?

His muscles were completely spent from the neverending marathon of a day, and he struggled to keep up with Maera. They had only just left the marina, and his arms felt like they were filling with cement. As the weight grew, he found it harder and harder to conjure the strength needed to make the next pull. The distance between them grew.

Maera continued to move with speed towards the empty blackness that cloaked the island in the distance. She flew across the surface of the water. Out so far ahead of him, she looked like she was standing alone on a stage, surrounded by darkness, under an invisible pale blue spotlight.

Evan wondered if he should just let her leave. He could just stop paddling and allow the night to fill the space between them. He could just let her go. Maybe they weren't meant to remain together now that she had the key.

While in the moments before he had felt so close and so connected, he now felt like the space between them was uncrossable. She was so focused on her rowing that by the time she noticed he was no longer right behind her, he would be so far behind. She would then have to choose between turning back for him and returning home. Doubt filled him, and he began to think he knew which she would choose. Maybe she was paddling with such fortitude in an effort to leave him behind anyway.

Of all the options - urging her to stay here with him, going with her, or both returning to their own worlds - he felt like the last was the most logical. But what place did logic have in love? He would never be able to fill the empty space left inside without her. Each pull of the paddle was like pulling a petal from a flower in the old "She loves me... she loves me not" routine. Let her go - stroke - ask her to stay - stroke - go with her - stroke - let her go - stroke - ask her to stay - stroke - go with her - stroke. He wondered what he would end on when he made his last pull to the island.

Maybe he was just too tired to care anymore, but before he could allow fate to decide, the fatigue in his muscles made the decision for him. Evan made one last pull against the water, and his kayak slowly coasted to a stop - let her go.

It's for the best, he tried to convince himself. Although he didn't believe it. So he allowed himself to be honest and admitted that he was just so tired... both his body and his mind...he was too tired to keep going. He didn't know what to do, so he just did nothing. Perhaps that is fate after all. Maera glowed faintly, ahead of him now by at least three football fields. She continued to paddle, and the distance between them grew greater. He turned to look back at the shore, which he could barely see behind him at this point. He figured they had traveled almost half the distance to the island by now. No wonder he was so tired.

He sat bobbing in the darkness, unable to decide his next move. He felt his face become wet before he realized he was crying. She was gone, and he knew it. He had let her go. "Stupid," he cursed aloud at himself. Overcome by the urge to leave his own skin, Evan set down his paddle and rolled his body over the edge of the kayak. The water bathed him in its warmth. He lay floating on his back, eyes open towards the sky blanketed with clouds, rocking gently on the surface, cradled. He willed all the stresses of the day to be washed away.

He was reminded of being a child. On nights when he couldn't fall asleep, he would call out to his dad with worry. With patient love, his dad would quietly enter his dark room and kneel next to his bed so that his face would be level with his. In a hushed tone, he would speak. "Shhh now, Evan. Your worries are too heavy. Set them free and let them float away." Starting at his feet, his dad would slowly stroke his son's legs and lead him in mediation. "Imagine you are lying on the warm beach with your eyes closed. Go ahead, close your eyes now," he would urge. Evan would reluctantly close his eyes, convinced that his problems were too big to wash away. His dad would continue. "Now feel the water begin to lap at your toes as the tide begins to come in. Feel the warmth flow back and forth, back and forth, over your toes, feet, ankles, and lower legs." His dad's voice would remain soft and low as his hands gently stroked back and forth to simulate the ebb and flow of the tide. He would continue in this way, working up Evan's legs. "Now feel the warm, gentle waves wash over your hips, across your belly, and down your arms. Feel the water flow back and forth, back and forth, back and forth." His hands would match his slow, quiet words. As if conjuring a spell, a charm would fall over Evan. He would feel as if he were no longer in his bed but instead floating on the warm surface of the ocean. He would allow himself to be lulled by the gentle rocking words and touch. His father would remind him to allow himself to be carried away, like his worries, on the ocean tide. Evan would be relaxed and asleep within minutes. It worked every time.

Here he was now, practicing the same technique. As Maera paddled further away, her light dimming from view, he felt his worries float away on the warm waters of the Gulf. Knots uncoiled from his shoulders. The throbbing pain in the left side of his back, where he struck the desk during the fight, eased. The weight from his arms floated away. The cramp in his belly vanished. He felt empty.

Water filled his ears, and he lay still, listening to the muted sounds. He could hear the sound of his pulse, each beat slow and steady. He focused his mind on the rhythm. Its consistent measure cleared his thoughts. For just this moment, there was no Maera, no key, no underwater world, no old man, no gun pointed at his face - just the woosh, woosh, woosh of his heartbeat.

The cadence was interrupted by a low growl building in the distance. His stillness was replaced by alarm. He pulled his body upright, rigid with attentiveness, and startled by the sound of a motorboat churning against the water. Urgency stampeded through him, and he rocketed out of the water, pulling himself back aboard his boat. He scanned the distance for Maera and was barely able to make out her faint blue glow, a tiny dot in the distance. He began to paddle towards her, pulled like a magnet against his control. He then searched the open water to determine the sound's direction of the coming powerboat. Speeding in from the north, he could see the red and green bow lights of a boat that looked and sounded like it was headed quickly towards Maera.

His previously leaden arms, now responded with such strength and intensity that he marveled at his own ability. Digging deep with each stroke, he felt the water move in huge scoops as his speed increased. He switched his focus from Maera towards the boat and back, trying to measure the distance. The boat was moving quickly, so he pushed harder, knowing he had to get to her first. "Idiot," he cursed again at himself, angry that he had given up. He was furious that he had allowed her to continue on without his protection. Somehow, he had convinced himself that he was acting in both of their best interests, but really, he had only been selfish. He had been tired and scared. He hadn't known what decision to make, so he had opted for the path of least resistance. Disgusted by his previous laziness, he worked hard now, determined to reach her before whoever it was on that boat did.

As he paddled harder and harder, the distance between them shrank but at a rate that couldn't be explained by his effort alone. He was moving fast, but so was she. Evan realized that Maera had turned back and was paddling with equal fervor towards him.

Despite the speed of the powerboat, Evan and Maera were able to reach each other before it reached them. Evan wished he could hide under the surface of the water when he saw the knife-like glare Maera cut at him. As their boats pulled alongside one another, she grabbed his wrist firmly and slapped the device against the side of his temple. His face burned from the strike, but also from his own embarrassment. With a tone, he had not heard from her before she demanded, "Where were you? What happened? Why were you so far behind?"

Evan dropped his eyes and stared down into the black water, unable to hold her gaze out of shame. "I... I..." his mind stammered knowing there were no right words to explain his cowardly actions. He knew she knew anyway. He could feel it.

"You gave up!" Her words were like a slap in his mind, harder than the one which had just struck his face. "Why did you give up?" Before he could answer, she swung her head sharply to the left and demanded further, "And now, who's that? What are we going to do?"

Evan looked up from the water and turned his attention to the boat barreling towards them. It was close now. Its engine cut off so as to drift up beside them. There was no escape at this point, so Evan weakly replied, "Nothing." The fight had completely left him. This time he knew without a doubt he had nothing left to bring. No anger, no fear. He felt nothing.

Maera swung her frustration back, and her grip tightened on his wrist. "Evan! We have to do something!" She shook his arm like a rag doll's. The force rippled through him like he was made of jello.

Completely flat, Evan replied, "I know. But I can't." He was empty. His lights were out, and no one was home inside. He felt like a tame zombie as he stared without blinking at the boat gliding closer. The water preceding it surged forward and bounced their kayaks. He was so limp that he would have fallen out of his boat had Maera not been gripping his arm so tightly.

"Evan!" he heard a voice call from onboard the boat. In that instant, it was as if someone had entered the darkened house of Evan and with the flick of a switch, turned on the lights. Hope was reanimated.

"Mom!" he responded, his body leaning forward, peering through the dimness to see if it could possibly be true. "Mom?" he called again, worrying that maybe he had just been hallucinating.

"Oh, Evan!" Her voice quivered as she replied back. "My boy. You're ok." The powerboat was now parallel with their kayaks, and his mom reached down over the side. Evan pulled away from Maera's grasp as he reached both arms up to wrap around his mom's lowered neck.

"Mom," his voice broke, and he buried his head into her curls. He breathed deeply, taking in her smell. Her deep aroma, like that of warm chocolate, comforted him as it always did. "Mom," he said again, ensuring she was real. He felt a strong but gentle hand on the back of his head, squeeze him in tighter and knew instantly to whom it belonged. "Dad!" Evan pulled away enough, so he could see both of his parents lean over the edge of the boat before him. A deep sigh poured from Evan as he relaxed deeper into the safety they both provided.

"You're ok, right?" His dad's low voice also cracked with emotion.

"Yeah, yeah… I'm fine." Evan took one more deep restorative breath from his mother's embrace before releasing her. "Are you ok, Mom? I know that guy hit you." He quickly added, "Ross is ok too, right?" His brother's head popped from behind his dad's shoulder. A big, goofy grin spread across his face as he nodded in the affirmative.

"Yes, sweetheart, I'm fine. Just a bump to the head is all. Nothing that won't be made better by time." She sounded so calm and reassuring, Evan couldn't help but believe her. "Ross is fine, too." A smile spread across her face.

"Fine enough to not be talking again, I see." Evan smiled back at Ross. He lowered himself back down into the seat of the kayak and turned towards Maera, taking her hand in his. Her head was turned sharply away from him, and he could see a scowl clenched firmly in her brow. His thumb stroked the back of her hand. He looked back up at his parents and said proudly, "Mom. Dad. This is Maera."

His mom covered her gasp with her hand but was unable to hide the shock as she whispered in response, "Oh my, Evan. She's more beautiful than I could have imagined."

Evan felt himself beaming with pride. He looked back towards Maera, smiling and nodding reassuringly at her. However, she didn't return his enthusiasm. "It's ok, I promise. We're going to be fine now," he insisted. He could tell she wasn't convinced as she cast her gaze downward and away like she was unsure of where to look. He squeezed her hand again and urged her to look back at him. "Maera, I'm sorry. I totally let you down. I know it. I was scared and confused, totally worn out. I know that's not a good enough reason, I do. Please let me make it up to you now. I promise it will be ok. These are my parents. They can help us. I promise I will protect you. I won't let you down again." Evan was thankful for the ability to communicate with Maera without words. He was glad his parents and Ross weren't privy to his affectionate vows.

Maera's icy hardness softened, and she turned to look at him. "Are you sure?" Her eyes still held a fearful concern. "They took the key before."

In order to prove it to her, Evan turned back towards his parents. "Mom and Dad, we have to help Maera get home. Please. It's so important. She's not safe here, and she has to return the key."

"Of course we'll help. Oh Evan, I just wish you would have come to us sooner. We've been worried sick." His mom's scolding tone was softened by her being thankful he was safe. "Come. Both of you, get yourselves onboard and let's develop a plan. It's not safe to be out here like this."

Evan turned back to Maera. Her eyes were still suspicious. Evan urged, "Maera, please. Let them help us. We need their help."

"Do we really? It's just a little bit further to the island. Once there, all I have to do is make my way back to the cave and take the key home." Her plan was simple, but she still sounded unsure.

Evan couldn't tell if she was unconvinced that they needed his parents' help or unconvinced that returning with the key was as easy as that. Regardless, he pushed at the crack he saw in her resolve. "But the old man is still out there. It was easy enough for my parents to find you glowing out here on the dark water. What if it had been him who had found you instead? What if it had been someone else entirely? It's just not safe." Another pang of guilt struck as he thought about letting her go alone, unprotected. He could see her resistance weakening, so he pushed a bit more. "You won't be safe until you're home again with the key. Let's not take any more chances."

She nodded consent. Relief washed over Evan as she turned and reached up to grab his dad's outstretched arm. Once she was safely aboard, his dad turned back to pull Evan up as well.

The five stood in a circle on the deck of the boat. His parents were unable to keep their gaze off Maera's luminous beauty as they tried to make sense of what they were seeing. Ross still smiled an unusually large grin at his brother. Evan nodded and patted Ross' shoulder. "Thanks for getting them. We needed help. I know you broke your vow and talked for me. That means a lot."

Ross nodded back. "It's no big deal," he responded, though they both knew it was. Able to joke again, now that they were all safely reunited, he added, "I just wish I had grabbed your communicator device to use on Mom and Dad, so I hadn't had to break my silent streak."

Evan smiled and shook his head as he sat down on one of the padded seat cushions. The relief of it was glorious. He slapped his hands on his thighs and exhaled deeply. "Ok, first things first. Who has some food? I'm starving."

Chapter 20

Upon finishing the third energy bar, Evan took a deep breath and rubbed his hands together. "Whew. I think I'll be ok now. Thanks, Dad." Maera was still nibbling on her first, spending more time on examining, rather than eating, the strange packaged food she held in her hands.

"Sure, I'm glad I still had them in my 'armageddon bag,'" his dad smiled in return. Then his smile straightened, he cleared his throat, and his eyes became serious. "Evan, we have to address the fact that you left without telling us today. Your actions had serious consequences. Aside from causing us to miss our international flight out of Miami, you worried us sick. We even called the police." Evan wasn't sure if his dad had paused for effect or if he was taking a deep breath to keep himself from crying. After an uncomfortable moment, he continued. "You need to be thinking of a way to make this right, Evan."

"Dad, please believe me, I know." He was embarrassed to be having this conversation in front of Maera. Even though she couldn't understand his dad's words without the communicator or without touching, he was pretty sure she got the gist of his dad's message. She was looking even more closely at the food in her hands, trying to avoid eye contact. No matter what world you lived in, everyone knew what it was like to be scolded by their parents. "I didn't feel like I had a choice," he added, sounding whinier than he had wanted to.

"Evan, you know you always have a choice." His mom's tone was softer than his dad's, but her gaze was more piercing. "We'd like to believe that you know you can come to us with anything."

"I know, Mom. I know," Evan muttered.

"We're just so glad no one was seriously hurt," his dad continued. "At least that we know of, right? How did you guys get away from that crazy man?"

"Well, it was Maera, really. She saved me." Evan reached to take Maera's hand into his lap. She sat beside him on one of the boat's seat cushions.

Without taking his eyes off of hers, he continued. "The guy had me down and was ready to end me, but Maera stopped him." Her head tilted slightly in modesty, but her eyes beamed with pride.

"Oh Evan," his mom covered her face at the thought but quickly regained her composure. She stepped forward and crouched before Maera, taking her other hand in hers. "Thank you so much." Tears filled her eyes. "Thank you for saving my son. I will help you in any way that I can." His mom's sincerity was so real. Maera nodded understanding. Evan could feel Maera's reservations melt away. She took her other hand from him and gave it to his mom.

His mom's eyes widened with awe. Her face lit up with wonder and Maera smiled in response. You would have thought Evan's mom was standing on the rim of the Grand Canyon or seeing her baby for the very first time. Everyone could see it. Ross nodded in understanding. Their dad leaned down beside her with concern.

"Bret, are you all right?" he asked his wife. Without saying a word, she reached back to grasp her husband's hand and lead it back to join with Maera's. But confusion remained fixed on his dad's face. "What? What's going on? I don't get it?"

Evan thought he understood and smiled. At least he wasn't the only one in his family who needed the communicator device. Apparently his mom had the same mysterious gift as Ross, but clearly, his dad was like him and did not.

Evan removed the orb from his own temple and looked down at it in his hand. It looked like a pulsing comb-jelly. He couldn't fathom how it worked, only knew that it did. He leaned forward, brushed his dad's hair aside, and placed it on his greying temple. Before he had a chance to question, the quizzical look vanished from his dad's face and was replaced by an expression that matched his mom's - astonishment. His eyes widened, his jaw loosened, and the corners of his mouth curled upward in a slight smile. Evan knew he now understood.

The three remained in a circle, their hands clasped together in the center, their arms like the spokes on a wheel. Evan could imagine the images that flowed from Maera to his parents as they stayed rapt during the passing minutes. It was as beautiful to watch as it was to hear the symphony. He could see his parents swell with emotion like the crescendo of an orchestral strings section. Surprise would strike their faces like a crashing cymbal. Several times his mom closed her eyes and smiled softly like she was listening to the light flute solo. His dad's head nodded in a rhythmic understanding as if the tympani was pulsing on the back row. And after a time, perhaps when the conductor had lowered his arms, his mom finally spoke. "How does this work?" Her eyes jumped from Maera's to Evan's to Ross' expecting an explanation.

Evan and Ross both shrugged their shoulders, but Evan spoke. "I don't know, but it's amazing, right? It's how they communicate."

Too captivated before now to notice, Evan's mom now reached up to her husband's temple and fingered the strange device. "Why does he need this to hear her, but I don't?"

Before he was able to respond, his mom was looking at Maera and nodding with understanding. Clearly, she was explaining, and Evan didn't want to interrupt.

Speaking out loud for the benefit of everyone not connected, she responded. "So I have to be connected with you to communicate, but I don't need a device because I'm a woman? Really? That's fascinating." She appeared to listen to Maera a bit longer before shock widened her eyes. She quickly swung her head in Ross's direction. She scrutinized him before looking back to Maera. "No way... he can communicate like this too?" Without pausing to get permission, she snatched the device from her husband's temple, placed it quickly to hers and then took both of Ross' hands. Tears streamed from her face. "Oh, how I've missed your voice, my love." She smiled and turned back to Maera. "Thank you. This is a lovely gift. You've given me more today than you could ever know."

Maera smiled and nodded. She didn't need to understand her words to interpret the meaning. A mother's love - that is universal.

"Hold on a minute." Evan's dad made a T with his hands, signaling a time-out. "I'm confused." He paused and with his eyes closed, shook his head as if trying to organize the swirling information in his mind before continuing. "I can communicate with Maera when I have the device. Mom can communicate without it as long as she and Maera are touching because she's a girl, but Ross has that gift as well?" He took a deep breath. "This is going to take me a second."

Chapter 21

After going around and around for what felt like hours, Evan's dad finally seemed to accept everyone's communication abilities. "Genius!" he exclaimed. "It's just pure genius! That's all there is to it."

His mom still wore the device, unwilling to give it back and lose communication with Ross again. His dad clearly understood how important it was to her because he didn't ask. However, Evan was becoming impatient to communicate with Maera again. "Mom, can I have that back, so we can discuss our next move?"

Reaching up to remove the piece, she replied, "Of course, honey. I'm sorry I've been hogging it. I've just missed hearing Ross so much," she added, as she squeezed Ross' shoulder. "You know I support you, Ross, but I did enjoy hearing your voice tonight when you were in the hotel room, despite the scary circumstances." Ross nodded. "Speaking of which, we haven't addressed that man and where we go from here."

Evan replaced the device and turned to Maera taking her hand. "Hey you," he heard in his mind as she smiled brightly at him with her eyes. He felt the familiar spark flash instantly between them.

Turning back to his parents, he said, "Well, the last we saw, the old guy was lying on his floor, out cold. I'm not sure how long he'll be out, though. Perhaps we should call the police and get them over there."

"Already did," his dad retorted. "When I got back to the hotel room and found your mom and brother recovering from a whack to the head, I immediately called the cops. Ross wrote down where the guy lived in the marina, and they headed there. However, when the police got to that guy's houseboat, and no one was there, they called us. We were worried sick that he had taken you and Maera somewhere. Your mom couldn't just sit and wait, so we borrowed this boat from the owner of the hotel and headed straight out here to look for you. Ross figured that if you were able to get away, you guys would be headed back towards the island. Thank goodness he was right and that we were able to find you safe."

"Wait. So you're saying that the old guy is out there somewhere?" Evan felt panic rise within him.

"Evan?" the worry returned to Maera's voice as well. He felt her squeeze tighter.

Refueled and a bit more rested, he felt more capable of handling challenge than he had been before. "It's going to be ok. They can help us now. I won't let you down this time," he reassured her, speaking out loud so his family could hear. These weren't empty words like before. He actually believed himself as well this time.

His mom reached out and rubbed Maera's knee. "He's right sweetie. We're here, and we'll figure out a solution together."

His dad reached in, nodding with confidence. "Of course. We'll all be ok, now that we're together." He shot Evan a glance as if to remind him that his risky actions from before hadn't been forgotten.

Ross reached in as well, connecting the five of them for the first time. "It's going to be ok," he added.

His mom and dad both reacted with shock, surprised they could hear Ross even without the communicator. Before they could question it, Maera was the one to offer an explanation. "We're all connected now."

Evan felt overcome. His love for his family and for Maera was so great, the connection with both so strong. He wondered how he could ever choose between them.

Chapter 22

"We really have to get you home, Maera." His mom spoke first. "I'm sure your parents are both beside themselves with worry over you being gone for so long."

"I know," Maera replied with downcast eyes. "But, I'm sure they're furious I took the key. As much as I know that I need to get home, I'm not looking forward to facing what awaits me." Her shoulders slumped at the thought.

"Oh, sweetheart... I'm sure your parents will be so relieved to have you home that it will soften most of the disappointment they may have over your choices. Take Evan for example. He would be in a world of trouble right now if we hadn't been just so relieved to have him back safe." She glanced at Evan and gave a playful wink before continuing. "Your parents want you to be safe, above all else. Believe me."

Evan smiled, pleased he was able to finally hear the conversation between Maera and his mom and also because he was so thankful for his parents.

"That doesn't mean you're off the hook, buddy," his dad jabbed. Although he had a smile on his face as well, Evan knew his dad meant it.

"Yes, but I won't be immune from the consequences for taking the key. I'm sure my mom won't be able to protect me from the law."

"The law?" Evan asked with shock. "What do you mean? Like jail?"

All eyes were on Maera as she sat nodding, eyes still downcast. Timidly, she lifted her face to Evan before explaining. "I took the most sacred treasure of my people from a locked case in our most protected temple. It's a big deal."

Instead of conveying words to communicate, she now shared images to help them understand. A large circular room with high, vaulted ceilings filled their minds. The walls seemed to emit the same ethereal glow that Maera did as if they were painted with glow-in-the-dark paint. The subtle light provided a magical atmosphere to the space that made it feel like the room was somehow alive. Rows of low benches spiraled around the room in a radial pattern like the inside structure of a mollusk shell. In the center, elevated above on a pedestal shaped like an elongated bloom, emitting the brightest light in the room, was the key. The four of them inhaled sharply in unison, moved by the resplendent image playing in their mind.

Evan thought about what it would be like to steal the Declaration of Independence. He acknowledged there would be no escaping the penalty for that, even if his mom was the president. Then the idea developed further as he realized the key was even bigger than that. He was unable to come up with one thing so sacred among all people on land as the key was in Maera's world. Chills ran through him when he understood the depth of the consequences she faced. Everyone in his family was nodding solemnly as they too came to the same awareness.

His mom was the first to respond. "No matter the trouble you've caused, your parents still need you to come back. It sounds like your people need you as well." She stroked Maera's hair in an attempt to help soothe the evident hurt. "You have the strength within you to do this. I can feel it."

Those words were just the right salve to assuage Maera's fear and worry. She sat taller, lifted her chin, and even smiled slightly. "I know you're right. It's what I have to do. I have to return the key. It's the right thing to do. My parent's need me. My people do as well. The key is sacred, I know that now." Her smile grew to include a twinkle in her eyes as she looked to Evan. He beamed back, enjoying the secret connection they shared. "Evan taught me that," she added.

Evan blushed at the display of affection that was exhibited between Maera and him in front of his family, but the embarrassment didn't suppress his boldness. He confidently blurted out, "I'm going with you. We can face the consequences together." He surprised himself. He hadn't planned it, but once he said it he knew, without a doubt, he would go with her. He wasn't leaving her again. Now that it was decided, he felt so much lighter, so much braver. He smiled, nodded, and said it again. "I'm going with you." He liked the sound of that.

Maera's eyes locked with his. Their connection was amplified greater than before, and everything around them blurred into obscurity. Without having to say a word, he could feel her agreement and excitement. In that moment, he knew he would be connected with her always.

"Evan... Whoa. Come on now, Evan!" his dad spoke slowly and raised his voice to get his attention. "You can't go!" He looked to his wife as if to ask, he can't, right?

His dad had clearly been expecting his wife's back up and was shocked when she replied quietly, "If you must, Evan."

"What? Bret, you can't be serious. I mean, be reasonable for goodness sake. Think about what he is saying for just a moment." The relaxed look on her face didn't change as her husband challenged and pushed back. "Our son... your boy," he corrected in an attempt to play to her emotions, "is telling us he is leaving to go to another world, got that, world!" He stretched the word to add further emphasis. "He is going to live with the mermaids, and you reply 'if you must.' Can you hear yourself? This is crazy." He could tell he wasn't gaining any traction with her, so instead, he turned his attention to Evan before continuing. "No! Emphatically, NO!" He surprised everyone by yelling the word. "You are not going with Maera. That's insane, makes no sense and isn't happening. No!"

Evan never had seen his father this flustered before. He felt a sense of relief at knowing where a bit of his own fire came from but was shocked by this new spark. Clearly, it was unfamiliar to his mom as well, and she attempted to soothe her husband. Turning towards him, she stroked his shoulder and said, "Peter, please calm down and let's talk through this rationally for a moment. We can't lose our heads over this."

He pulled back from her with an appalled look on his face. "You must be kidding me! You actually expect me to give Evan a hug and send him on his way to live who knows where with who knows who under the ocean. I mean seriously, listen to how insane this all sounds." He broke away from the group and stomped the short distance to the bow of the boat with his hands clasped on both sides of his head as if trying to keep it from spinning off.

Unsure of what to do next, the four were left staring at each other. Surprising everyone, Ross spoke the next words aloud, "I'll go with him." All eyes swung towards him.

"What?" Evan shot back at Ross. His first impulse was to object. Maera was his and his alone. This was his destiny, not Ross'. A calm wave surged through him, like a force from outside himself, which stopped himself before he did. Did it come from Maera? His mother? Both still had a hand holding each of his. Instead of resistance, he felt relief. Perhaps having Ross with him in an unknown world would be just what he needed. They had traveled this world together, sharing all of their discoveries. It seemed fitting that they would explore the next together as well.

Before he had more time to consider it further, their dad shouted back, "Have all of you lost your minds?" Covering his mouth with his hand in an obvious attempt to prevent himself from saying more and hurting anyone with his words, he sat down on the front edge of the boat.

Stunned and unable to formulate a response, the family stared back at him with worried eyes. With a quiet gentleness, Maera plucked the communicator device from Evan's temple and walked over to where his dad sat. She gently brushed aside his hair, placed the orb beside his brow and knelt before him, taking his hands within hers. Minutes passed in silence as the two held a private discussion. Evan's curiosity burned to know what they were talking about. He actually had to clench his tongue between his teeth to keep from interrupting. His mom must have sensed his emotions too because she placed a calming hand on his back and traced circles to mollify him. Just when he thought he wouldn't be able to hold back any longer, Maera and his dad both turned toward Evan and nodded in agreement. Whether she fully understood the accord, his mom nodded as well, and it was silently decided. Evan and Ross were going with Maera.

Chapter 23

The silence was broken by the churning sound of a motor in the distance. All eyes swung to the east and began scanning the dark horizon for any indication from where the sound might be coming. Evan pointed towards the north. "There, see the lights on that boat. It's moving towards us." Hand in hand, Maera, and Peter quickly walked back to reconnect the group. "Dad, quick, turn off the bow and stern lights," Evan said in a hushed tone. "Maera, wrap this over your head and shoulders," he added, grabbing a towel from the floor of the boat. He lowered his body into a squat and pulled the family down with him, in a feeble attempt to hide on the open deck of the boat out in the middle of the Gulf. As they did, his dad reached towards the center console and flicked the light control off. "Perhaps whoever it is will just pass by without noticing we're here." He wanted to believe his own words, but his pulse quickened when he considered who it might be racing directly towards them, closing the distance at an alarming pace.

Maera's face was filled with fear as she pressed closely beside Evan. Again compelled by the seriousness of the situation, Ross spoke aloud. "Do you think it's that crazy old guy?"

"There's no way he'd be able to know we're out here!" his dad countered.

They all paused for a moment, hunched low on the boat, considering all the possibilities. "Mom, Dad, who did you say you borrowed this boat from?" Evan asked. Struggling to contain his desire to blame, he added, "Did you tell him where you were taking it?"

His parents held a private discussion between themselves with just their eyes. Evan marveled at the connection they shared, had cultivated over the years, and smiled at the similarities that were budding between Maera and him. They had it too, he thought. While it may not be as honed as the communication skills that Maera and her people employed and obviously lacked any additional devices, his parents could read each other's minds as well, in their own way. The two came to the same conclusion simultaneously, and both replied, "Oh, Evan, yes."

His mom continued further, "We didn't consider the consequences before now, though. Before we jump to any conclusions, let's consider this may be an unrelated incident. That boat could zip right past us. We don't know for sure it's coming for us."

Evan hoped his mom was right. However, it didn't seem that was going to be the case. The oncoming boat was barreling directly towards them at an alarming rate. It would be upon them in under a minute, Evan thought. Ross must have been thinking the same thing as well because he blurted out, "Why are we just hanging around like sitting ducks? We have a boat, let's get out of here." Without waiting for anyone's approval, he jumped into action and started up the engine. Everyone scrambled to find a hold and keep from falling off as he slammed the boat into high gear and turned sharply away from the oncoming boat.

"Ross," their dad yelled above the roar of the engine. "I don't think we're going to outrun him." Looking back over his shoulder to gauge the distance that was shrinking between them, he added, "Plus, where are you headed anyway?"

Ross yelled back, "Anywhere but here."

The clouds that had before blocked out the night sky now brought with them a gusting wind, evidence that a storm was building. Both boats bounced high across the light chop like stones skipping as they flew. Evan looked back over the stern of the boat and knew his dad was right. The pursuer was zigging and zagging in response to Ross' evasive turns, in an obvious attempt to overtake them, and it was working. Evan loved Ross' enthusiasm and shared his desired to do something, anything, but was worried about how this would play out. Ross had taken the helm on several boating trips in the past. He knew the basics of boating, but he was certainly no stunt racer. The boat hit the water at an odd angle, jarring everyone onboard.

Evan recovered his grip on the cleat and looked to see the distress mirrored on his mom's and Maera's faces. He turned back to his brother. "Ross, this is crazy. Trying to outrun a faster boat won't end well. It's just too dangerous, and you know it," Evan was shouting loudly to be heard above the rushing wind, the churning motor and boat's hull slamming against the water. Either Ross couldn't hear him, or he was choosing not to because he stayed facing forward with the boat at full speed. Evan knew he would have to offer some alternative if he was going to change his brother's mind. "Let's just stand our ground and fight. It's five against one. We can take him." Not wasting time to consider the plan all the way through, Evan scrambled to set his alternate plan into action. He yelled to his dad, "Look for a flare gun, some rope, a knife - anything we can use. Ross, stop the boat. Everyone lie down."

Ross nodded and cut the engine. Their boat lurched forward against the cushion of water that instantly slowed their pace. The driver of the other boat hadn't anticipated them stopping so suddenly and had to quickly turn and slow his boat to avoid slamming into the back of them. Evan could barely make out the old man's bushy white beard through the darkness that separated them, confirming what they were up against. He knew that he would have to gain the upper hand first if they had any hope of getting away from that nut-job. He was sure the old guy would have a gun, and that would be enough to even out the five to one odds. The approaching boat had more momentum and skimmed past their boat's port side.

Just as the old man was throwing the throttle into reverse to bring his vessel to a stop, Evan sprung up and over the side of his boat onto the other. His quick action took the old man off-guard, and he was able to grab him by the shoulders and slam him to the deck. With one knee jammed into the man's flank, Evan used his body weight to pin him and keep him down. The man's body twisted and whipped around beneath him like an angry snake. Thankfully, Ross was right behind. He straddled the man's legs and looked like a bull-rider taking his turn at the rodeo. With a hand on each of the man's ankles, Ross struggled to contain the bucking beast. Kicking both legs in unison, the old man launched Ross' hips high into the air, but Ross didn't lose his grip. "Dad, grab some rope!" Ross yelled over his shoulder.

Maera and their parents were scrambling on the other boat, frantically lifting seat cushions and opening hatches in search of something they could use to restrain the man. "Peter..." their mom cried, her voice filled with worry and fear when she came up empty-handed.

"I'm looking, I'm looking," he responded with equal emotion.

Maera continued to silently, rapidly search, but her face did not hide her panic.

The old man growled and spit as he struggled. "Get the hell off me!" he bellowed. He was able to twist his upper body and wrangle his right arm free. He wasted no time in swinging a hook punch across Evan's jaw. The force knocked him back against Ross, who then lost his hold on the man's legs. Before rebounding to a standing position, the man delivered a swift kick with his heel into Ross' exposed side. The man pulled a gun from the back waistband of his shorts, cocked it and alternated his aim between both boys who lay crumpled, holding their wounds on the boat's deck.

Evan felt the left side of his face expand with heat. He could taste the metallic flavor of blood washing over his tongue as he used it to search for the source. He found a long tear on the inside of his cheek. He could feel his heart pulsing through his teeth, echoing loudly inside his head. Sparks of light exploded in a fireworks display across his field of vision, and he blinked rapidly to try and clear his sight. When he did, he saw the old man standing above him, breathing heavily, pointing a gun at his head for the third time tonight. The man's sneer made Evan's skin crawl.

"Evan! Ross!" their mom screamed before covering her own mouth in terror. Maera stepped along-side and took her free hand. Tears began streaming down both of their faces. Their dad stopped his rummaging but not before he found a mooring fender attached to a long rope underneath the last seat cushion. He discreetly hid the line and bumper behind his back as he turned his body toward the old man. He stood silently, calculating the next move, shifting his gaze between his huddled boys and the maniac pointing the gun at them.

He finally spoke, holding one hand up in a peaceful gesture. "Let's everyone calm down." He paused and took a deep, cleansing breath, letting it out slowly for effect. "I'm sure we can work this out without anyone getting hurt." His voice was steady and calm.

"It's a little too late for that, pal," the old man spat back with vitriol. "Your boys here have just boarded my boat without permission and attacked me. I'm only acting in self-defense, to which I'm entitled, seein' how they're on my property and all." He glared across the distance that was growing between the two boats as they drifted apart on the slow current. He briefly took a turn pointing the gun at the other three as he continued. "I don't take too kindly to acts of piracy. You can't just go storming onto someone else's boat and start attacking." The gun swung back to Evan and Ross who were peering up at him. "You boys need to learn your lesson. Obviously, your parents should have taught you better manners." He shook his head from side to side as he continued. "Breaking into people's places, taking things that ain't yours..."

"Are you kidding me?" Evan interrupted. "You stole that key from us in the first place!" he screamed, rising up.

"Evan," his dad warned in a low tone, but he was useless at preventing Evan from continuing.

Eye to eye now with the old man, Evan glared in defiance at the gun pointed at him. His breath rapid from fear and anger, his shoulders and chest were rising and falling in quick succession. The old man's brow tightened further in response. "Boy," his slow southern twang plucked at the vowel bending it in two. "You best mind me. I'm done playing games. I'm getting that key back. Whether or not you end up as fish food... well, I suppose that's up to you, isn't it?" The two continued to stare. Invisible rays of hate lasered between them. Through clenched teeth, he growled, "I suggest you sit yourself down. Now!"

"Evan..." a small, melodic voice pleaded across the distance between them. Hearing her enunciate his name for the first time caused such a stir in him that it broke Evan's face-off with the man, and he turned his softened gaze towards her. Her eyes pleaded with him, tears still streaked her cheeks.

"Please..." his mother's voice now added. She too looked at him, eyes imploring him to stand down. He couldn't hear either of them say anything more within his mind, but he knew exactly what they were asking of him. His mom's dark eyes, pulled slightly downward by age but still full of beauty, begged fiercely without sound.

Unable to resist the two people who held the most power over him, Evan nodded in acquiescence. He turned back to the man with his head bowed. He slowly lowered his body down to his hands and knees on the boat deck. He turned and saw Ross' worried eyes before the old man boasted, "Well, now, that's more like it." He heard the sickening laugh of a sociopath and then felt heat and pain flash across the back of his skull as the man cracked the butt of the gun across it.

"Evan!" He heard his mom and Maera scream in unison. He teetered on his hands and knees before collapsing under the weight of his body, which seemed to increase exponentially every second. Struggling to keep from passing out, he lay on his side and watched what happened next through his tunneling vision.

Like kernels of corn in a hot pan unable to contain themselves under the increasing pressure, Ross, Maera and his parents all erupted at once. Ross lunged forward with such speed and force at the man's feet that he was able to lay him out flat in one strike. Simultaneously, Maera dove overboard. Her light illuminated the dark water under the man's boat as she swam to the other side. She then pushed with such strength that the gap that had developed between the drifting boats closed. Even before Maera was able to complete her task, their dad wasted no time in running down the length of his boat deck and bounding up and over the platform at the stern. His leap seemed super-human, allowing him to fly the distance and land on the old man's boat. With the rope and fender still in hand, he swung it around his head in a lasso motion, generating as much momentum as possible before releasing it at the man's head. The old guy had only just begun to bring himself up onto his hands and knees after Ross had knocked his feet out from under him, but the whipping force was so great, and their dad's aim was so spot on, that he was again slammed flat to the boat deck, out cold. Their mom went to work immediately onboard their own boat and retrieved a second white bumper from underneath the seat cushion where her husband had found the first. The boats were now side by side, thanks to Maera, so his mom could simply step up and over to the man's boat. She quickly secured the old guy's hands behind his back with the length of line attached to her fender as he lay unconscious at her husband's feet. Their dad then used his rope to hog-tie the man's feet to his hands.

They were just finishing tying him up when Maera gracefully pulled her drenched, glowing form up and out of the water. Unable to resist her transcendent beauty, all eyes turned to her. She stepped over to Peter and took his hand. Evan didn't understand why she would go to him first until he saw his dad reach up to his temple to remove the device that he still wore. Maera smiled, giving his hand one last squeeze, then turned and walked toward where Evan was lying.

Her light filled Evan's vision as she crouched beside him. She placed her cool, wet hands upon him to secure the device to his temple. He could feel himself rising back up from the depths that had just threatened to pull him into dark unconsciousness, unlike that of his attacker who lay beside him. "Oh Evan, oh Evan, oh Evan," he heard her voice in his mind, full of relief as she placed kisses on his forehead, cheek, and chin. She paused. Her face just inches away from his. "I was so scared. That was the third time today that I thought I was going to lose you. The thought of..." she broke off before continuing. "I just can't bear it. Before last night, I didn't know a world with you in it. Now, I can't imagine a world without you." She lowered her face and placed her mouth against his. Her cold, damp skin was in such contrast to the electric heat that burned within him and between them. She pulled away from the kiss, and it was like her magnetic force lifted him to a seated position.

His parents and Ross circled around in a big group hug. "Evan," his mom sobbed, pressing her face into his hair. She breathed him in deeply like she was refilling herself with him, before she pulled back. Taking his face in her hands, she scolded, "You acted so foolishly." She closed her eyes and kissed his forehead. She shook her head and then opened her eyes and added in a softer tone, "You acted so bravely."

"You both did," his dad said in addition, beaming at both of his sons. "I'm so proud of you."

"I'm the one who should be proud," Evan protested. "You guys were like a gang of superheroes working in perfect unison. It's like you all planned that."

Ross scoffed. "We did, you buffoon. Did you forget we could all communicate without talking? While you were busy with your stand-off with the old guy, we were formulating a plan of attack. Dad was wearing the device, Mom and Maera were holding hands, and I was over here, doing my best to try and hear them all without touching. I was focusing so hard, trying to make it work, and somehow, it did. Maera choreographed the whole thing." Turning toward her, he added, "Your plan was great, by the way. I still can't believe you were able to push that boat so quickly and all by yourself."

Without feigning any modesty, Maera nodded with thanks. "Yeah, I've had some practice swimming," she jabbed with a smile. Everyone responded in laughter, so obviously relieved the threat of danger had passed. "I'm just glad it all worked out." Her thumb stroked Evan's hand, and her smile remained. "Are you sure you're ok?"

Evan rubbed the back of his head and could feel two knots under his damp curls. "Yeah. I've got a pretty hard head. I'll be alright."

"Yeah, I'd say you're hard-headed for sure." His dad tousled Evan's hair and winked teasingly at his son. "You nearly scared the pants off me, standing up to someone with a gun like that. I'm sure glad things ended the way they did."

Evan winced and pulled away from his dad's playful hand. "I said it was hard, not indestructible." Evan's smile proved to everyone that he would be just fine. "What's next, though?"

The group paused in shared silence as they all looked from one to the other around the circle they had formed. Wondering who would speak first, his mom finally nodded and then spoke. "We have to get Maera and the key home." She swallowed, holding back her obvious grief over the next part. Her voice cracked as she continued. "And we say goodbye to the boys." She forced a smile but couldn't hide the tears streaking her face.

Their dad looked down at their mom's hand, which he held and stroked. Tears filled his eyes as well, but he nodded. "Yep." Before being able to say more, he sniffed, took a deep breath, and raised his head to his sons. "It's time they head off for their next great adventure.'" He smiled now, his eyes wet still. "When I think about all the many amazing places we've discovered together as a family over the years..." He choked up. He took another ragged breath and looked to his wife with such love in his eyes before continuing. "I just wish we could go with you."

"Dad..." Evan began but wasn't sure what to say next. Luckily, his dad protested.

"No, son, no. That's not what I meant. We know we can't go with you. Your mom and I knew this time was coming. I'll admit, I didn't think we'd have to part ways this soon, and I obviously never considered this scenario." He paused and tilted his head in the direction of Maera, giving her a wink, so she knew he meant no hard feelings. "But honestly, my sons," smiling at Ross and Evan, "we have always wanted this for you. We always hoped you would both embark on your own journeys - make your own discoveries, and you have. You are." Looking again at his wife, he held another silent conversation with just his eyes. His smile grew even bigger; all his tears now dried up. "We couldn't be more proud of you than we are right now. We know you're ready for this. So let's go. It's time."

Done with talk and ready for action, their dad stood, brushed his hands down the front of his shorts to straighten out the wrinkles, and then clapped his hands before initiating orders. "Ross. Set the motor on this guy's boat to idle speed, and turn him towards land. We'll let him motor back to shore where he can work out his own fate from there. I'm sure by the time he makes it back, the cops will be more than happy to help him out." Ross nodded and hopped into action. "Evan, lead us back to the island we camped on last night. Let's do this thing."

Struggling to hold back tears of his own, Evan quietly nodded in response. He smiled at his dad, proud of his blessing and acceptance. However, when he turned to his mom, he couldn't contain the surge of emotions, and the tears flowed. She had always had that effect on him. He could never hide his true feelings from her. "How am I supposed to leave you guys?" he managed to say with a quivering voice.

"Oh Evan," his mom said through exhalation. "My sweet, sweet boy." She leaned in and kissed the top of his head again before looking him squarely in the face. "You were born for this. You're my fearless explorer, always have been. A man of action - that's who you are. You've been all around the world. You've climbed high peaks and traveled into deep canyons. Never once were you scared. This is no different now." She reached to brush a tear from his cheek. "Just think, you get to explore somewhere no man has ever been."

"No *land-man*," Evan corrected with a soft smirk.

She closed her eyes and nodded once to accept his playful correction before continuing. "You get to dive into a world of mystery. I can't imagine a better next step for you than this."

"Plus, it's not like this is forever. No mom would just send her boys away without a plan to meet back up." She smiled and smoothed a wild curl into place behind his ear. "One month. We'll meet back on the island's beach in one month. Do you understand?" Her eyes shifted between both Evan and Ross to make sure they had an agreement. "If you guys aren't out there waiting, then your dad and I are coming in after you." She winked at them both.

Her face beamed back at him with confidence, but Evan still shook, wracked with emotion. "But Mom," his jaw quivered as he spoke. "I won't have you with me. I..." He couldn't continue through his tears.

"I know, my babe." His mom's voice was so tender, so reassuring. "I won't be there this time, but you and Ross will have each other. " She paused and reached her other hand to stoke Maera's face. Her smile grew even bigger as she added, "And you'll have her."

Evan turned towards Maera and was instantly calmed by her glowing beauty. Embarrassed by his messy show of emotion, Evan struggled to stop his tears and calm his breathing. It was time for him to pull it together, he reminded himself. He took a cleansing breath and nodded, looking back at his mom. "You're right." Another deep breath. "One month. Deal." He took one more breath and then smiled. "You're always right." He turned again to Maera. "I have you now." Squeezing both their hands, he stood tall and nodded one last time. "Let's go."

Chapter 24

Evan cut the engine, and their boat drifted silently to shore. He hopped into the ankle deep water and turned back, holding a hand out for Maera. She took it and lowered herself down beside him. Ross bounded over the bow and pulled the boat up onto the beach. Their dad slipped himself over the edge onto the sand and reached back to lift their mom down with both hands. The couple hugged in a long embrace as if they were the ones who were about to say goodbye. His parents pulled back from one another and again held silent counsel before nodding in secret agreement. His mom's curls whipped in the wind, that was now blowing with a steady force. It would be raining before the boat pulled away, carrying only the two of them.

Maera squeezed Evan's hand. "They're lovely," she said, smiling. "It's beautiful to watch them communicate."

Evan turned and smiled back. She was right. He was lucky and knew it. That's what made it so difficult for him to leave them.

"It won't be forever, you know." She squeezed his hand again, and her eyes twinkled.

"I know. I know." He said, bobbing his head in agreement. "It's just hard." He paused, determined he wouldn't cry about this again. "I'm just going to miss them so much."

Ross surprised him by slapping his shoulder and speaking aloud again. "Ah, brother. Don't worry. You'll have me." He raised his eyebrows, and his eyes twinkled.

Evan groaned back. "Ugh, don't remind me." He rolled his eyes in a teasing response but felt lighter at the thought. The weight of his heartache was eased by his brother's support. The sound of his voice was a novel comfort.

Their parents walked over hand in hand. "Ok, Evan. Show us where this cave begins. We'll say our goodbyes there."

Evan turned and extended his arm with his hand outstretched. "After you, Maera. Ladies first." He winked.

"Ok, but this is the last time. You're going to have to get used to the other way around, my friend." She winked back.

Maera began the procession through the mangroves. Reminded of the last time the family made the arduous journey through these dense trees, they were thankful that this time the wind was enough to keep the mosquitos at bay. Despite the clouds covering the light from the moon, Maera's glow was enough to make negotiating the tangled path easier. After a short trek of ducking beneath low limbs and climbing over rising stumps, they arrived at the entrance to the cave. At first glance, it appeared as only a small depression in the earth, barely distinguishable by its darkness. Maera stopped and turned around.

"What? This is it?" their dad asked, surprised that such a modest hole could lead to a magical world.

Maera silently nodded. Their mom nodded back. "Ok," she said in almost a whisper. "I love you." She grabbed Ross and pulled him close to her. Her hands gripped the back of his shirt tightly, and she buried her face in the space between his neck and shoulder. His dad's arms reached around, and they stood enfolded for a long moment. When they released, all three were smiling.

They turned now to Evan. Together, his parents encircled him with their arms. In unison, they said, "We love you," and that was all. It had all already been said, and Evan was glad for it. He didn't want to part with tears, and he knew if they had said anything else, he would have cracked again, all of him spilling forth.

He smiled and replied. "I know. I love you too. Thank you for this. Thank you for everything." It wasn't enough to express his gratitude for all they had given him, but he knew nothing ever would be.

They turned to Maera and hugged her together. She naturally folded into them, like she had been doing this her whole life. Still holding on to one another, they pulled back to look into each other's faces. They stood that way, silently communicating until they all nodded once in accordance.

Without looking back, Maera lowered herself and crawled into the hole, out of sight. Evan was surprised by how quickly it all happened. He stood there, feeling as if he had a choice to make, and he realized that he did. Because she didn't turn back to make sure he was following behind, Maera had left it up to Evan. She was allowing him to ultimately decide - stay above with his family or come below with her. He looked at his parents, who stood smiling with complete composure. They appeared totally neutral. They too, were not influencing him in any way. Then Ross shrugged, lowered himself into the hole as well and also was gone. Evan thought he saw his mom hold her eyes closed for something longer than a blink when Ross disappeared. If she was breaking inside, her poise did not betray her.

Evan glanced between his parents and the cavern entrance. His breathing quickened along with his pulse. Stay or go? Stay or go? The question bounced in his mind. Then, he remembered. He had already made the decision. He would go, and he did.

Note From The Author

Word-of-mouth is crucial for any author to succeed. If you enjoyed the book, please leave a review online—anywhere you are able. Even if it's just a sentence or two. It would make all the difference and would be very much appreciated.

Thanks!
Amanda

Amanda Mahan is a native Floridian who wishes she was a mermaid. She settled for the next best thing and wrote a story about one. Now after years of writing for her office job, she has taken the plunge to become a novelist and is working on the sequel to her debut novel *Mermaid's Key*.

Thank you so much for reading one of our **Young Adult** novels.

If you enjoyed our book, please check out our recommended title for
your next great read!

Camp Strange by Renee Perez

"*Camp Strange*, in fact, is the best thing ever."

–KIRKUS REVIEWS

View other Black Rose Writing titles at
www.blackrosewriting.com/books and use promo code
PRINT to receive a **20% discount** when purchasing.